Basal Ganglia

ALSO BY MATTHEW REVERT

A Million Versions of Right
The Tumours Made Me Interesting
How To Avoid Sex

Lazy Fascist Press
an imprint of Eraserhead Press
205 NE Bryant Street
Portland, Oregon 97211

www.lazyfascistpress.com

ISBN: 978-1-62105-127-5

Copyright ©2013 by Matthew Revert

Cover Art Copyright ©2013 by Matthew Revert

Edited by Cameron Pierce

Proofread by Vanessa Rossetto and Robert Hamilton

All rights reserved. No part of this book may be reproduced or transmitted in any form or by any means, electronic or mechanical, including photocopying, recording, or by any information storage and retrieval system, without the written consent of the publisher, except where permitted by law.

All persons in this book are fictitious, and any resemblance that may seem to exist to actual persons living or dead is purely coincidental or for parody or satirical purposes. This is a work of fiction.

Printed in the USA.

Basal Ganglia

by Matthew Revert

A Lazy Fascist Love Story

"it seems they were all cheated of some marvelous experience which is not going to go wasted on me which is why I am telling you about it"

—Frank O'Hara

1.

He is Rollo. Rather, at one point he was assigned the name 'Rollo' and was referred to as such. Rollo's name now lives beyond memory. Unuttered in longer than time recalls. A name signifies identity. Something Rollo has lost. The complex information packaged in the label 'Rollo' is dead data. Why voice a name when the need to differentiate one from the other disappears?

A second person shares existence in the fort. This second person has also been assigned a name, but like 'Rollo,' it has lost its voice. In a world of two, who is addressed if not the other? What use is a name?

She is Ingrid. Unlike Rollo, Ingrid remembers her name. Although unvoiced, its memory survives in writing. Ingrid wants her name and protects it. The death of memory within Rollo calls toward what little memory Ingrid still has, wishing to consume her morsels of identity, rendering both he and she empty. Ingrid knows Rollo's name. It features in her secret writings as regularly as her own. This way, a part of Rollo survives, even if he does not know it. Even if she does not want it. Within Ingrid, the data comprising each name fights against complete corruption.

He is Rollo and she is Ingrid.

...

Lost in the repetition of another in a never-ending set of maintenance tasks, Rollo feels the peace of insignificance. Within the endless hunger of the pillow fort there is no outlet for significance. His hands perform with the intricacy of

Bharatanatyam dance, forever reinforcing the fort walls. There is a drive to protect, but the danger is ambiguous. Commitment has a way of becoming purpose and Rollo's commitment to protect Ingrid has become the sole arbiter of reality. There are always slackened blankets to tauten, or pillows to plump. Maintenance never ends, a fact that comforts Rollo, solidifying his purpose. A projection of external danger must remain stoked with new fear, lest it ebb toward complacency. Complacence has no place within the illusory movement of stasis. When one commits to upholding the illusion, stasis becomes purpose.

Rollo has concluded as an individual. Charting his history suggests nothing about his present as the divide between then and now consists of an ambiguity. One suggesting the existence of something long-faded. Even a memory still burning with its inspiration possesses fraudulence. Rollo was once an accumulation of incorrectly remembered experience. It would be inaccurate to suggest Rollo has no concept of his pre-fort self. He understands intellectually how he moved from where he was to where he is, but the impression of experience is absent. What may be considered a remnant of memory lacks any tangible core, only succeeding in further clouding a grasp on what might have been. For Rollo, the consumptive power of an eidetic experience is an unknown concept.

It is in this context Rollo's daily life is carried out. As is typical for those engaged in what consumes them, he bemoans the encroachment of hunger and sleep. Anything severing him from his self-imposed duties is regarded with frustration bordering on contempt. His life has been sacrificed to the fort's need, which he satisfies from the Parietal Chamber. Within this Chamber are the myriad building tasks he invents, in various stages of completion. Wherever possible, maintenance work is performed here and transported to the area of need once complete.

He is replacing the stuffing in a pillow from the Prefrontal Chamber. His eyes are no longer required when performing this task. Hands subservient to muscle memory divorced from conscious understanding, moving in patterns. There is a time before pattern when all that exists is imperfect sequence. Sequence that alters with increased understanding. Steps removed. Steps added. Steps streamlined. Eventually the steps are forgotten. Merely performed. The pattern becomes its own existence and Rollo is a simple conduit. This dissolution from conscious engagement suits Rollo. He exists in clouds that float above his performance. Within these clouds, his mind reaches toward the next task. The next pattern.

As his hands perform – one gaping the emptied pillow, the other filling it with new stuffing – Rollo's eyes survey the Parietal Chamber. He marvels at the light bleeding through from the Occipital Chamber. A flawless level of luminescence. Detail is revealed as needed. His many projects sit around him. Some forgotten, most simply waiting their turn to be forgotten. He must devote his time to essential maintenance, but sometimes wishes there were an opportunity to explore non-essential projects. Fort beautification. Luxury. A prototype bed sits to one side. One made of higher quality materials that adapts readily to individual contours. Something Rollo believes Ingrid would appreciate. The belief has no evidence to support it. There is a possibility Ingrid communicated her discomfort at some point. He engages in a simulacrum of recall that retrieves illusory moments. He makes a mental note to clarify Ingrid's position regarding a new bed and immediately forgets it. The new bed is an item of luxury and must remain abandoned.

The pillow's innards have been replaced. Rollo considers the old stuffing strewn about his feet and cannot bring himself to dispose of it. There was a time when this grey, deflated filling was pristine. When it impregnated the pillow with the promise of comfort. There is no possible maintenance for the stuffing. Rollo knows he cannot imbue it with newfound life. The stuffing is a casualty of the maintenance process. Replaced and forgotten. Keeping it would serve no purpose. He is best to dispose of it in the Medulla Shaft and continue as though it never existed.

He collects it. Hugs it to his body and feels within it a desire to expire. He walks to the Medulla Shaft and lets it fall. The pieces float and interact with one another as if to say *goodbye* before disappearing into darkness.

The knowledge he has to let go is much worse than the moment it happens. We invent attachments that feed on past loss. Silent fear finds its voice in objects we keep, reaching a volume we cannot ignore when *goodbye* arrives. Deflated stuffing can be more than its form. Deflated stuffing can become a manifestation of every forced goodbye. The manifestation finds resistance when the object is discarded. As the stuffing becomes immersed in the collected waste of the fort, he has already forgotten there was a time where he cherished it. A time when it reached toward past goodbyes. The newly plumped pillow is studied closely. It requires no further work. He moves it to an area of the chamber designated for completed projects. Until he delivers the rejuvenated pillow to the Prefrontal Chamber, the job's conclusion lies in wait. Rollo withholds this final step. The memory of this success will disappear upon delivery, and this memory is one he would like to experience a while longer. Before it becomes the numb expanse of familiar mental nothing. He will deliver the pillow when it is time to eat. As food sustains him, the memory will disappear and Rollo's nothingness will fill with the next task – the nightly atmospheric readings. Numbers will be deciphered, recorded, measured and analyzed. Discrepancies will be investigated.

Satiation via repetition. A comforting sense that no process meets its end. Rollo is a warrior gorging on the excess of minutiae. His insignificance redefines significance. Turns it around. He inflates the smallest unit of measurement until it possesses enough size to break it down further.

...

Unless they are eating or sleeping, Rollo and Ingrid never occupy the same place. The fort has dictated the two should exist in separation, as though unified presence will invite discord. The discord refuses to acknowledge itself. They have been together since the age of thirteen. Both share the same birthday. Neither remembers when that is.

Sometimes Rollo worries he will forget Ingrid. Most days pass without her entering his mind. On occasion he will take a break to try and remember her name. 'Ingrid' is a word that has died inside him. It is not rare for panic to thrive when the erasure of 'Ingrid' from Rollo's lexicon is reflected upon. The dream sense of falling shifts his equilibrium, forcing him down, absconding with his breath. Light becomes difficult to discern and he must wait for it to flood back in. He strives to forget that he has forgotten.

He has taken to sitting in the Cerebellum Chamber and trying to write letters to Ingrid. A one-sided epistolary attempt to keep Ingrid alive within him. He forgets so much. Written language has escaped him. There are words he sees when his eyes are closed, but these mental words cannot be conveyed in written form. He wishes everything could be communicated in numbers. Numerical values can convey untold complexity. Numerical values can calculate the world. Yet there is no number that equates to Ingrid. If there is, he has not managed to find it. The divide between the fading Ingrid in his mind and the physical entity he understands to be Ingrid increases. Rollo believes in the language-bereft letters he tries to write. They are a bridge, something that exists beyond him but because of him.

These reflections bother Rollo. There is always maintenance that must be done. Reflection is a punishment. The antithesis of action and progress. Maintenance must be done.

2.

Expansive love exists within Ingrid deprived of outlet, growing with the weight of unexpressed feeling. Feeding on her perpetual fight to suppress everything it wants to be. She cannot remember what she looks like, but often wonders if she is beautiful. How could such love exist where there is no beauty? There are mirrors in the Occipital Chamber, but they are used for surveillance. The mirrors reflect like any other, but they are already married to a process, and Ingrid has no desire to become a part of it. She believes in the possibility of her beauty because she cannot recall anything she considers ugly. Everything possesses beauty within the details of its details. Ingrid knows details. They are the atoms that cling together and form all things.

Meditation is found in the sensation of her hands moving over the contours of her face. Skin surprises her. Touch ignites her. A beard pushed through her chin some time ago. Cobweb-thin at first, but evolving with the assistance of time into something thick and strong. Her face wears this masculine trait with feminine pride. Everything her body exhales into existence is something of which to be proud. How could any manifestation of her body be incorrect? Mental fingers sift through memories and find nothing. *If women have no beard, then why do I have a beard? I am a woman and I have a beard, therefore women have beards.*

Ingrid sits in the Prefrontal Chamber, turning a pencil in her hand, watching it with interest. Observation is Ingrid's art. Like Rollo, she lacks connectedness with any aspect of herself before the fort. Observation replenishes mental content, replacing forgotten memories. The pencil in her hand is not merely a means to an end. The pencil is a buzzing swarm of electricity embedded with history. It came from somewhere. An idea turned reality. A factory line somewhere at some time gave birth to it. Somehow, from the whorl of machinery, it emerged and found its way to this moment. When Ingrid observes this pencil, she imposes a history upon it. Each imposed history is an effort to impose a history on herself. Unlike Rollo, she longs to be more than now. For Ingrid, everything preceding this moment in time informs this moment in time and every moment to follow.

It is in the Prefrontal Chamber that Ingrid feels most comfortable. She casts her gaze from the pencil turning in her hand to the notebook sitting before her. The pencil wears a newly sharpened point. A point she will blunt with words. There are so many words living inside Ingrid and she wants to write them all. She wants to explore every possible sequence of words. She wants to know how words relate to one another. If words exist in conflict, she wants to observe the conflict.

Most of Ingrid's words, in one way or another, find their way toward Rollo. 'Rollo' is a word she will never admit she remembers. Ingrid would never let Rollo read her words, but most of them are devoted to him. She seeks honesty with her words and often feels guilt at the contempt they reveal. During the brief moments they share, it is difficult for Ingrid to look at Rollo and for him to look at her. It often feels like an unspoken game between the two – looking everywhere but at each other. She wonders if the two should attempt a conversation that probes deeper than Rollo's maintenance narrative, but knows it is unlikely. She fears any attempt to probe beneath Rollo's most exterior layers will reveal love within him that matches hers.

Ingrid has noticed an evolution in her writings. They extend beyond words and have started including diagrams. An unknown fascination with concentric circles has developed. Ingrid's hand seems compelled, beyond her intervention, to draw circles within circles within circles, concluding with dots wanting to be smaller circles. Were it possible, she would shrink herself down. She knows what looks like a dot must contain vistas of space in which to draw more circles. If only she were small enough to experience the extra space she knows is there. This space is wasted.

Beneath the circles she writes about her desire to shrink. Longing has been building within her for some time. Days are passed wondering what this longing might be, but instead of answers, she finds only an amplification of the longing. At its worst, she envies Rollo and wishes to lose herself in the same menial activities that occupy the totality of his mind. She thinks too much, an activity that at times strikes her as absurd. What purpose do thoughts serve when they lack a means by which to manifest?

She runs a hand through her beard and attributes to each bristle an identity filled with complexity and wisdom. She wishes Rollo had a beard and wonders why one does not grow. What lurks beneath the surface of his skin preventing it? Does he ever envy hers? Her hands would like to feel Rollo's chin, but are terrified of touching him. The concentric circles on the page beckon her toward their center.

She writes the next in a sequence of numbers on the top-right corner and makes her way toward the Frontal Chamber. The Frontal Chamber belongs to Ingrid. Rollo does not know she spends time there each day. He believes this chamber disturbs Ingrid, but he is wrong. Within this chamber, darker than the others, Ingrid feels a symbiotic connection. Whatever might have occurred here during the construction of the fort married her to this chamber. In this marriage, Rollo has never had a place. This chamber is an opportunity for Ingrid to try and understand what it means to be her, severed from any dynamic attached to Rollo.

Within the Frontal Chamber is a cavity beneath the floor. She often feels as though the fort belongs to Rollo, which is why this space is so precious. By lifting the layer of blankets that comprise the floor, she is able to gain access. In this cavity Ingrid files everything she writes. She dares not stay inside the Frontal Chamber too long as time has a way of escaping when one is immersed in the self. When Rollo returns from his maintenance for supper, it is important to Ingrid that he find her in the Prefrontal Chamber – like always. It is a pattern he has come to expect and Ingrid knows he needs his patterns. Ingrid's own pattern relies on the successful execution of Rollo's. She allows herself to luxuriate in this forbidden space for a moment after filing the latest writing. This chamber feeds her in a way that defies expression. Thoughts that terrify her elsewhere fill her with comfort here.

When she returns to the Prefrontal Chamber, she wonders how long she has been gone, then immediately counters this with nonchalance. All that matters is Rollo is not back yet. The tryst between Ingrid and the Frontal Chamber remains their secret. For all Ingrid knows, Rollo has a space just like it for himself. She hopes he does, but knows with a great deal of certainty he does not.

3.

A limbo exists between the waking and sleeping world. The waking world has no place in the silent darkness. We exchange the day for a transition into a facsimile of death that masks complex explosions of biological function unfolding within. These functions wait for the mind to disappear. The limbo between wake and sleep is a ceremony that mourns the loss of another day.

Rollo's childhood suggested insomnolence, but his sleeplessness was a considerable act of will. In a time when Rollo still had the ability to remember, he remembered the wooden crib that housed him each night. Placed down so gently, as though he were in danger of breaking, onto soft bedding replete with infancy's understanding. His arms reaching for the arms that had just released him. Wet lips pressed against his forehead, leaving a dampness that cooled before disappearing. The warm, orange hue of lamplight designed to grant him peace.

The lips.
The light.
Then loneliness.

In this crib, the room contorted beneath the lamplight's gaze. The light removed familiarity and replaced it with danger. His body responded to confusing messages uttered by the contorted environment, telling him sleep must come. Sleep must take today's life and leave you helpless. Rollo feared the room around him, but feared surrendering himself to the room much more.

His blankets were tucked so tightly only seizures of movement would convince them to yield. When Rollo managed this, he burrowed beneath the blankets, remaining awake and hidden from sight. The world was different beneath the blankets. In the presence of such danger, this small gesture calmed him. The space was intimate and unique. It was his and granted entry to no one else. When he was not there, the space stopped existing.

Consumed in this world of blankets, Rollo remained awake, assured in the knowledge when sleep finally stole him, it would not be by choice. Of course... sleep always stole him, sooner or later. He would wake each morning tucked tight by loving hands. Hands that assumed his position beneath the blankets a mistake that needed correcting.

Night's inherent danger evolved to mean many things to Rollo as his age and awareness grew. No matter the evolution, the central concern remained devoted to extending the limbo. Sleep remained an enemy. Waking life was a composition of the self, performed with certainty. Sleep signaled a pause in the composition and became free improvisation performed by the subconscious. This was a performance refusing to pay attention to any malignance that wished Rollo harm.

Waking life, although preferable to sleep, became a source of fear all its own. As Rollo accumulated more worldly experience, he saw the pernicious hue of infancy's lamplight gaze draped across every facet. Each day held within it, just below the stretched skin, threat and harm. It occurred to Rollo sleep did not introduce danger into the world. The danger was always there. The limbo between wake and sleep allowed Rollo to stay both alert and protected.

...

A child builds a fort for many reasons. Common to most children is a drive to understand a world dictated by them. Within the walls of these basic structures are eruptions of imagination. A blanket draped over two chairs transcends its constitution, becoming limitless. It is a structure that garners meaning via the hands that build it. The eyes that behold it.

Rollo's nighttime reveries soon oriented themselves toward the simple notion of a pillow fort. He would gather and form what to him were grandiose strongholds. His bedroom became a blanketed womb mapped with tunnels and nooks. It went beyond a familiar childhood pastime and became a statement of intent. The structure longed to break free of Rollo's bedroom and consume the entire house. Within the heart of this shambolic architecture resided Rollo himself. Whenever his presence was not required elsewhere, he was in his fort.

School was important to Rollo. He was able to absorb many practical and theoretical worlds of experience that could benefit forts of the future. His hands were blessed with natural aptitude, able to solve puzzles of construction with detached dexterity. His mind was capable of deciphering the language of computation and engineering. The school environment was a source of potential danger that was outweighed by the skills it provided. Divorced from social concepts, his mind was given permission to focus on selfish improvement. His avenues of study extended far beyond the limited curricula students were expected to abide by. The structured imposition of learning was enslaved to equality, almost scornful of those who had hungrier minds.

Fellow students formed indistinct patterns Rollo had no interest in. The students in turn regarded Rollo with confusion and unnamable fury. In groups people devolve and subsume into a malignant mass. The mass distills into collective will guided by the lowest common denominator. The mass exhibits the fury of its most furious. The confusion of its most confused. Negativity swells and bucks, growing with the ease of weeds, choking out individual traits into voiceless morsels, pathetic and weak. This mass feared what the possibility of Rollo said about them. Rollo, without casting a thought in their direction, had stripped each one beyond nudity and revealed the weakness beneath the skin. The horror of being ordinary. In their ordinariness, they combined to become something less than ordinary. As one, they wore fear as courage and directed increasing disdain toward Rollo. The atmosphere was thick with jealousy and self-doubt, but Rollo never noticed. There were more important things in which to direct his concern.

Ingrid existed as a part of Rollo long before he became aware of her. She was often a member of the spiteful mass and knew she became a part of it with too much ease. When removed from the jumble she felt enriched, as if participation in the collective will diluted her as a person. Who was this Rollo that inspired so much weak rage? She moved in cycles of knowing and unknowing. Figuring the peculiar boy out and finding larger questions within her solutions.

Ingrid divorced the mass when she could no longer cope with the weakness it made her feel. In this gesture, she inspired a lesser form of disdain from the mass. Rollo's existence drained too much of the disdain's resources to attend to Ingrid in a satisfying way. Unencumbered, she watched Rollo through her own eyes. It became important for Ingrid to understand who this boy was and why he inspired so much jealousy and fear. He was someone immersed in his own trajectory and whatever it was, there was an aura of importance surrounding it.

This clandestine dynamic persisted for some time before Ingrid felt compelled to introduce her presence to Rollo's trajectory. She engaged. He accepted and returned the engagement.

"Hi," said Ingrid. "I'd like to introduce myself. My name is Ingrid."

Rollo stared into her eyes, trying to understand what it was they conveyed. In possession of new feeling beyond words. Feeling that could only be understood via feeling.

"Hi, Ingrid," said Rollo. "My name is Rollo. It is nice to meet you."

They found words to share and became connected to each other. Rollo extracted a portion of himself and gifted it to Ingrid. She held it close and in turn allowed Rollo a portion of her. They nursed this portion of the other, allowing it to bloom within them. What they shared felt more than love. Their hearts pumped each other's blood.

When Ingrid was first introduced to Rollo's bedroom fort, she intuited its importance. This was more than a structure that Rollo sought refuge in. This was a manifestation of all Rollo was. He had erected his own heart and invited her inside. The knowledge Rollo had dredged from life was directed here. Understanding the danger her presence in the fort might represent, she embraced Rollo and became another blanket in which he could hide. He turned in exploratory tumbles before swimming to her depths, where safety existed in untold abundance.

…

The intimacy of pre-sleep's limbo exists in its vulnerability. It is fed by solitude and grows with exploration of the reflexive self. Rollo handed Ingrid an invitation to his personal space. Rollo did not need to explain himself to Ingrid. When light became dark, she was waiting at the fort's core. He saddled up behind her and shuddered with the unknown. In their silence, he could hear the thud of another's heart, the exhalation of gentle breath. The limbic screech of colliding thoughts. In this space Rollo knew his safety was tied to the beautiful creature pressed against him. Their future was bound. His cells were merging with hers.

Each night, separate from any reality expected of them, the two would float through the pre-sleep limbo. They added further burrows to the bedroom fort and moved through them like blood through veins. Rollo became aware of Ingrid's thoughts merging with his. He would voice thoughts originating in Ingrid that had not yet been spoken, believing them to be his own. Rollo understood Ingrid was now in possession of his thoughts too.

Ingrid and Rollo. Start. End. Circular movements. Spun on the same spool and blending their threads into something stronger. Individual fears set aside for shared fear. The limbo pushed away everything unbound to them.

School's hateful mass continued to engorge and longed for a tangible manifestation of their disdain toward Rollo. He had not dwindled beneath them. He punished the mass by thriving in spite of them. A representative approached Rollo, blocking his movement, ensuring the mass would not be ignored. This collision startled Rollo. Who were these people and what was their business with him? The hands of another, shaking with physical violence, held him in place. How could such nameless hate exist? He motioned to move forward, the dreadful hands overwhelming him. These hands were not just owned by one hateful boy. They were owned by one seething, hateful mass. He was reminded of the hands that left him alone in the crib of his infancy. What right did uninvited hands have upon another person?

Ingrid, ensnared by a different set of hateful hands, was pulled from Rollo's side. Their thoughts telling the other to remain calm. She fought against the hands, but they possessed a strength she did not. Rollo turned to help Ingrid. Ingrid turned to help Rollo. Both turned away from helping themselves. One of the hands holding Rollo balled into a shaking fist and, with horrific efficiency, introduced the concept of deliberate pain to his body. Again. Again. Parts of his structure were breaking and voiding. Ingrid lunged toward the fist. Her lunge was truncated before she could help. Her body was pulled in the opposite direction, bleeding into the asphalt. A heavy foot pressed her in place while the wheezing pain of Rollo escaped him, too blunt to resonate.

The mass had fed. Rollo was left to fall beside Ingrid. They writhed toward the other's pain and found the sustenance of embrace. They both thought such terrible things. They both agreed on a course of action. It was the only future that had ever made sense. They had so much work to do and there was no one else capable of doing it. The world around them was a ferocious storm of endless danger.

Anatomy of the Fort

On a logistical level, the development of the pillow fort is one of incalculable complexity. From genesis to conclusion, the construction process, which in some ways defies any sense of true conclusion, took 25 years and was executed by Rollo and Ingrid alone. It was developed without the aid of a plan; rather it branched naturally from a central core.

The geographic location of the fort was chosen at random from a selection of several unfrequented areas. The absence of topographic choice lowers the risk of the fort's discovery, which Rollo cites as an added security measure. The unknown nature of the locale minimizes Potential Premeditated Predatory Activity (PPPA). PPPA considerations dictated the fort should reside underground and construction work should commence from a central core deep enough below the earth to reach a parent rock soil horizon. Construction branching from the central core should not extend above the illuviated subsoil layer, which allowed for a protective tunnel separating the surface from the entrance of the fort.

Rollo christened the central core 'The Cerebellum,' which inspired a naming convention consistent with brain anatomy. 25 years of construction resulted in a series of eight distinct areas (including the cerebellum) encased in a dura mater-inspired outermost layer. High quality linen materials were used wherever possible during the construction process – a characteristic that has maintained. It is assumed, for reasons related to structural integrity, linen is not the only construction material used. However, it is the only material visible.

What follows is a breakdown of the fort's chambers including their essential function.

MEDULLA SHAFT

The Medulla shaft runs the length of the fort and concludes at the deepest level of the earth surrounded by a hollow. It is the only component that penetrates the dura mater layer with one end connecting the fort to the surface and the other used to eliminate waste, which is broken down with the aid of a biological acidic agent in a polder-lined hollow. It is the primary arterial when moving from chamber to chamber and the only component predating the construction of the Cerebellum Chamber. It is analogous to a hallway and used to maximize airflow that enters the fort via a series of vents that circuitously stretch toward hollows near the earth's surface. It sits at a 33 degree angle, which allows for easy navigation.

THE CEREBELLUM CHAMBER

Located toward the base of the fort, the Cerebellum Chamber was the first built and is considered the structure's mainframe. During the construction, Rollo and Ingrid developed the techniques necessary to ensure all branching chambers could be built. A highly developed understanding of pre-electronic analog computing allowed Rollo to fill this chamber with a gear-driven calculation device. Modeled on a steamless version of the analytical engine, the analog computation abilities of Rollo's device relays atmospheric information within all chambers to a series of punch card readings, which are then converted to numeric values. These readings can be used as an early warning system by revealing potential faults in the fort's architecture before they occur. This device has been credited with preventing the occurrence of any serious structural damage from forming. In the absence of any known threat, it cannot be determined if this credit is warranted. All operational functions on Rollo's device must be performed by hand as human exertion is its only known fuel source.

THE OCCIPITAL CHAMBER

Due to the growth of a luminescent schistostega pennata moss, the Occipital Chamber is the source of all light in the fort. The origin of the light this moss reflects is unknown and the intensity of the luminescence far exceeds other examples of the species. Despite attempts to plant the moss in other chambers, it has been unable to thrive. Once removed from the surface on which it grows, the moss maintains its luminescence for some time, albeit at a lesser intensity. This allows for the illumination of the other chambers, however the moss must be replaced regularly. When necessary, the schistostega pennata can be used as a food source – this is avoided where possible. Via the careful placement of mirrored plates, the Occipital Chamber also serves as the fort's panopticon. All other chambers in the fort are visible from this chamber as long as vision occurs at the appropriate angle. The threat of Potential Unmediated Predatory Activity (PUPA) is contained via regular surveillance from this chamber.

THE PARIETAL CHAMBER

Conceived as a workshop, the Parietal Chamber is where all functional items of convenience are constructed and/or fixed. Residual luminescence from the neighboring Occipital Chamber allows for a light level that has the psychological effect of maximizing tactile ability and diminishing physical signs of fatigue. The highly specific conditions within the Parietal Chamber ensure it is also utilized as an infirmary should the need arise, which given the low risk of pathogenic infiltration is rare.

THE CENTRAL SULCUS EMERGENCY TUNNEL

This emergency tunnel separates the Parietal and Frontal chambers and was conceived as a panic room. In the event of a security breach, this area can be locked down, protecting anyone within. It is capable of dispersing infectious spores that will be distributed throughout all surrounding chambers incapacitating potential risks. Functionality of this process is purely theoretical as, to date, no such infiltration has occurred. In the event of this system's failure, the spores have been selected to merely incapacitate those that come into contact with it. The effect lasts an estimated 48 hours, in which time infiltrators must be removed from the fort. The Central Sulcus Emergency Tunnel is also used as a storage area and acts as an alternate means of access to all but the Cerebellum Chamber.

THE FRONTAL CHAMBER

Since the completion of the Frontal Chamber, it has rarely been used in any functional capacity. The reasons are ambiguous beyond Ingrid citing the presence of negative residual energy she believes could be harmful. Although not outwardly susceptible to this potential energy, Rollo has abided by Ingrid's request. Particular ambiguity surrounds knowledge regarding what this energy is a residue of and if it actually exists. Was it present beneath the earth prior to the fort's construction, or did Rollo and Ingrid introduce it? Whatever the answers may be, the questions ceased being asked long ago and avoiding the Frontal Chamber is now abided by without reflection. Generic maintenance duties have been performed in this chamber when necessary.

THE PREFRONTAL CHAMBER

The Prefrontal Chamber could be described as the living quarters. All food prepared within the fort is consumed here. This is also the chamber where Rollo and Ingrid sleep. Experiments sleeping in other chambers have resulted in unusual psychological disturbances. Atmospheric readings from the Prefrontal Chamber are markedly different from the others and remain relatively static. It is not known why the properties inherent in the atmosphere here are conducive to psychological stability, or at least what Rollo and Ingrid consider psychological stability to be. Of all chambers in the fort, the Prefrontal Chamber is the only one Rollo and Ingrid occupy at the same time with regularity. The closest ties to standard notions of domesticity reside here.

THE SYLVIAN GROUNDWATER IRRIGATION FISSURE

The Irrigation Fissure channels surrounding groundwater deposits into three cisterns that sit between the dura mater layer and the fort's chambers. Each cistern collects water of different mineral and temperature properties and distributes them via bamboo piping when a manual faucet is activated. The system was developed by Ingrid and is maintained by Rollo. The properties of the different water sources are naturally determined within the earth. Water obtained from the earth surrounding the southwestern area of the fort (toward the Cerebellum Chamber) has a tendency to be warm (with an average temperature of 88 degrees Fahrenheit) and perfect for bathing purposes. Remaining water sources are much cooler and used for all other purposes. The bamboo piping is routed through the base of the Medulla Shaft so as to utilize the pre-existing dura mater penetration without the need for further penetration. Grey water is treated with an acidic powder derived from deliberately spoiled food and disposed of via the base of the Medulla Shaft where it breaks down the fort's waste matter. The gas that results from the breakdown of this waste matter is released via a series of vents and absorbed into the earth.

4.

Unattended cracks yawn open and nothing is born perfect into this world. The blemishes of being allow for meaning by introducing perfection to strive for. The cracks that prevent our perfection need not start in gapes and rives. Most cracks flirt with invisibility, fooling our structures into believing their own integrity. In these hairline cracks the strongest diseases can grow. A relationship is successful when the inevitable hairline cracks, however invisible they may be, are acknowledged. It is easy to ignore inconvenient discrepancies. They do not call attention to themselves. They reward your ignorance by offering fleeting moments of extended comfort. For disease to strive, it must evade the host's intervention.

Rollo and Ingrid entered the fort with married purpose. Their love destroyed the possibility of space existing between them. This union bore no trace of the pathogenic orchestrations conducting disease. The unattended cracks were there, waiting with a statue's patience. Fertilizing pathogenic soil and sprouting illness. A relationship wants to destroy itself and will work toward this end. When two lovers first meet, a destructive sequence begins. This sequence is easily interrupted during the embryonic phases. When all one wants is to be seen as expanding perfection in the eyes of the one they love, we eradicate all disturbance and move forward with well-intentioned fraudulence. Our weaknesses are suppressed into a place hidden from the other. Cracks, fed by weakness, fraudulence, and self-protection, grow just beyond perception's grasp. Rollo and Ingrid were not immune. Their greatest mistake was assuming they were.

In the context of a world to shun, Rollo and Ingrid were bound. Their desire to withdraw from the world encompassed and became them. The role played by the world in this dynamic was overlooked. Construction of the fort was an endpoint, separating them from the world and dissolving their dynamic with it. The separation was achieved with such success that the world no longer provided a foil to kick against. They had subtracted meaning from their life and were ill-equipped to replace it. They were left alone, inextricable and in need. Lost to each other and unfamiliar with themselves. Memory lost its shape. Then it lost its form. Finally… its essence. Nothing existed to replace what was taken. When Rollo and Ingrid forgot who they were, there was only the isolation of now. The cracks became so large they could not face them. Both chose escape. Both chose an opposite direction. Two halves of one is still one and one.

...

"Have you seen my hairbrush?"

Sometimes when Ingrid talks, Rollo forgets to respond. He is too busy listening to the sound of her words rather than the meaning behind them. Often when Ingrid speaks, it is not to get a response from Rollo; she is reminding her inner voice she has an outer voice. She lets her words float like plankton, allowing Rollo time to comprehend them, not knowing how much time is appropriate. She wonders if the question is one she would like a response to and decides that it is.

"Have you seen my hairbrush?"

Rollo is listening now. The question makes sense. The combined words form a meaning. He cannot figure out why Ingrid requires her hairbrush. The level of light in the fort does not lend itself to vanity and of what importance is one's appearance without another in which to appear? It is unlikely Ingrid's desire to neaten her hair relates to Rollo's gaze.

"Why do you want your hairbrush?" he asks.

Ingrid does not answer. She has forgotten the question along with any relevance she once attributed to it. Some days Rollo and Ingrid forget to talk to one another. The act of verbal communication often strikes them as an unnecessary diversion from their own thought processes. Comfort resides in the safety of mutual silence. On occasion they will force a conversation. Ingrid will politely ask Rollo for a status report on the fort and he will provide details about various maintenance tasks recently performed. With scripted precision, this conversation will reach a muted apogee before winding down to nothing. Rollo will then ask Ingrid about the records she claims to keep, of which she will say little. Ingrid will abort her role in the conversation and worry about her hidden writing. It does not warrant too much concern. She can feel Rollo's emptiness in his every movement. Something beyond agency drags him from one checkpoint to another.

Ingrid clears Rollo's untouched plate.

"You should eat more than this."

Rollo was not aware of the plate until his attention was directed toward it.

"I think I will eat now."

The plate is placed before him once more. The collection of raw fungi and moss refuse to inspire appetite, but food exists to be eaten. He no longer considers the possibility of taste. Food is simply a mass of energy preventing his stomach from experiencing the discomfort of hunger. It provides the fuel his body requires to continue working.

Ingrid sits before her bureau. The day has made considerable steps toward its conclusion. While Rollo busies himself with the nightly itinerary Ingrid feels compelled to write a letter. Rollo never questions her about what she writes. He believes everything relates to the fort, including Ingrid's words. To Rollo, what Ingrid writes is simply data pertaining to whatever it is she spends her day doing. The pencil is blunt but not unworkable.

With every line, she pushes the pencil tip closer toward its demise.

Dear Rollo,

If I do not write these letters, I will forget you. I read your name over and over, and sometimes wonder how it connects to you, or if you are even the person I am writing these letters to. Sometimes I worry you have found these letters, but how can that be? That would mean you comprehend my existence when you turn away, and I do not believe that is true. You no longer have the capacity to comprehend what is not immediately before you. I think I prefer it this way.

I do not know how long we have been here, but it is a significant amount of time. At least it feels that way. I know no other time. This fort is my eternity. I have connected with myself more deeply than I ever thought possible. I am beginning to understand my DNA and listen to the special histories it reveals. I sense every change that occurs within, no matter how infinitesimal. I can even feel myself aging. I mourn the death and celebrate the birth of each cell. I have come to learn that I care about certain cells more than others. Do you ever feel this way? Have you ever looked at your hands and noticed the atoms of which they are comprised? I have started paying attention to my atoms and, like my cells, there are some I like more than others.

Do you ever write to me, Rollo? If I were to search, would I find undelivered letters addressed to me? Some days I am comforted by the thought of you reaching out to me, but most days, the possibility terrifies me. Honesty compels me to admit I have simplified you. I am thankful you have not given me reason to believe otherwise. I have deconstructed you into a rudimentary amalgam of machinery designed to perform basic functions. You have been stripped of complexity, because complexity is the foundation upon which unwanted love can cling. I need to believe that what I see in you is the extent of what there is to see. Aspects of myself that do not love you dominate me.

I have become aware of a truth, one that may apply to everyone, but I can only speak for myself. I am not one person, Rollo; rather I am a disparate series of selves that combine to form who you used to know. Each self is imbued with characteristics that take turns helming my whole. I have taught myself to find distance between them and me and have managed to observe, but not control, them. From what I can ascertain, there are at least twelve versions of me that reside within my shell. There may be more, but I can only speak for what I have found. Let me try and explain the role of these selves as far as I understand it. Each self possesses a distinct personality, much like I would attribute to my whole, only these selves remain largely unchangeable unless coaxed by the other selves. Some selves are weaker than the others and more susceptible to influence. What I understand as mood fluctuation is really just a different self, or set of aligned selves, taking control.

The selves within me are not defined by clear-cut emotions. There is no self completely concerned with sadness for instance, even though some of the selves appear sadder than others. Each self possesses a level of complexity that leads me to believe within them lurks another set of selves, but I cannot verify this. The more I understand about myself, the more there is to understand.

I love you, Rollo, but it has been a battle – one that I'm slowly losing. For love to develop between two people, I believe one of our selves must form an instant connection capable of bypassing all logic and self-protection. It is this capacity for instant love that can gradually win over the more discerning selves. One of these selves loved you a great deal, Rollo, and still does. She introduced the love response to the other selves and slowly found ways of converting most of them until I was consumed with love for you and could see nothing else. What you need to understand, Rollo, is while this self loves you so very deeply, there is another self that has always hated you. I believe this hate exists in all relationships at some level. Watching in patient silence for a moment in which it may interject. When a relationship is successfully executed, this hate is rarely permitted a voice. Its moments of domination are thwarted by the greater power of the loving selves. Most of the time one never suspects the existence of this hate until the beholder has an opportunity to come forward, but do not be fooled... this hate is always there and ignorance feeds it. It is a sleeping elephant.

The self that hates you is as devoted to its cause as the self that loves you. Our living situation has allowed my hate to gain prominence. For as long as my memory permits me to recall (perhaps before), my hateful self has sought to convert the others and, it pains me to say, has managed to succeed. As time goes about its business, more selves give in to the hate. Some of these versions of me are pitiful, and all too willing to shed the love they felt for you. With each new convert, the hate grows in strength and is recruited to work on the others. All that remains is the solitary self that introduced the rest to the concept of loving you. This difficult target has become the most treasured of all. Each converted self knows they cannot convert this remaining self, so instead they devote their time to killing it. I do not even know if this is possible. It seems to me my selves are inextricably linked, and killing one will entail killing all. Maybe they hate you so much that this sacrifice is worth it.

Ingrid

5.

Ingrid summons Rollo after they have eaten, a gesture which confuses him. In a severed past exists a time where one summoning the other regularly occurred. Implicit in the arrangement were a series of mental calculations where one would try and ascertain the potential cause of the summons. Tone of voice, word choice, and body language were used to determine the gravity of the situation. To Rollo, Ingrid appears different, and there is nothing within him with which to understand that difference. No projection can be made and predictions are returned without content.

Ingrid sits with legs pressed together and hands spanned across knees. Her head is directed toward an area of no concern, which she stares beyond. Rollo considers her posture and concludes it to be one of aversion. He supposes the aversion is directed toward him, but is not confident enough to trust it. When she grants him her gaze, it is fleeting, barely enough to acknowledge his presence. He attempts to maintain his, but without return, the gaze disquiets him, so he makes a point of looking everywhere Ingrid is not.

He sits before her, legs crossed like an obedient student. Silence exists between them that must be bridged.

"You wanted to talk?"

Ingrid shifts in her seat, disturbed from her inner world. Rollo contemplates leaving the situation and busying himself with maintenance work. He allows his question to sit unanswered and contemplates the work he could be doing. There is a sheet in the Occipital Chamber that has been thinning. As a chamber residing toward the fort's exterior, the importance of the task is elevated as it relates directly to their continued security. Sheets forming all outer walls must meet a minimum thread count requirement otherwise environmental conditions outside stand a greater chance of infiltration. Of the sheets in Rollo's stockpile, none currently meet the thread count requirement, therefore replacing the Occipital Chamber's expired sheet will entail reinforcing a sheet of lower thread count – a task that will be a significant time investment. Rollo must find a way to schedule this task around his daily duties. By requesting that his body clock wake earlier, and working during the lunch break, enough time can be found to approach the task with an appropriate level of care. He considers going to bed later than his body clock prefers, but worries such a significant reduction in sleep will diminish the focus required and ultimately act as a hindrance. This conundrum is a source of joy Rollo turns over in his mind to examine every angle. Angles are questions that do not demand answers. Each can be explored as much or as little as curiosity dictates. Rollo dances from angle to angle, indulging each new set of possibilities they inspire. Each angle serves the additional purpose of distancing Rollo from Ingrid.

"I want to have a baby."

Ingrid's words shift focus from Rollo's escape. Her words mean something inapplicable to his context. The word 'baby' requires that he upgrade internal software in order to understand. He attributes the word to inexplicable otherness. Something residing so beyond concerns of the fort process that its existence is questionable. Imagery is called to mind that becomes lost in spectral dissolves of quasi-understanding.

"Did you hear me?"

He stares at Ingrid, disturbed by the distraction of her presence. She wants to enact a change, the importance of which resulted in this summons. Something has penetrated their pattern and recalculation has become necessary.

"You want to have a baby?"

He repeats her words, hoping this will result in understanding their weight. His pink hand appears before him; dark purple webs of vein glow below the surface. The hand, now separated from Rollo's cognition, sweeps across his face. Over his shoulder. His breast. Traveling downward and resting on the peak of his belly. The ripple of gastric contortion investigates his palm, pulling its essence within. He feels what Ingrid's words mean before he comprehends them.

"You want to have a baby," he repeats. The words are no longer dressed as a question.

Ingrid locks her eyes on Rollo, an inescapable gaze he feels trapped within. His neck seizes and returns the gaze against his will.

"Is this something you're comfortable with?"

Rollo understands this question as one divorced from an answer. Ingrid's gaze is telling him the time has come to have a baby. His decision is not one of whether he will allow it; rather it revolves around his willingness to participate in it. The baby is a foregone conclusion. He attempts to understand the mechanics of making a baby. A baby is the result of two physicalities coming together as one. Surely Ingrid has no intention of instituting such an impossible process.

The potential repercussion such an addition to the fort may have entails a need for Rollo to align himself closely with whatever events are set to unfold.

"How shall we proceed with this?" he asks.

Ingrid finally unlocks her gaze, content her desires will be fulfilled. Moving about the solvency of affirmed headspace, she stands and feels the straightening of posture. The absolution of lungs enjoying unhindered breath. The conceit of something resembling purpose.

"I have spent some time considering this." she says. "The baby should be the result of us both. Made from the fort. An embodiment of who we are."

In contrast to Ingrid's affirmation of self, Rollo shrinks into portents of disquiet. A spike of concern unsettles his composure. Ingrid wishes to steal from the fort and make a baby forged of theft.

"I will knit the baby," she continues. "You will gather material of the highest quality. Material used in the fort's construction and maintenance and I will knit them into a baby. Our baby."

Sought words cannot be found. Rollo wonders if the words he seeks exist at all and if so, do they possess the meaning he wishes them to possess? He is left to agree without substance and wonders what baby might result from Ingrid's handiwork. He feels it should be his job to knit the baby. Anything built within the fort and of the fort should occur via his hand. He cannot recall ever having knitted anything, though his hands feel capable of performing the act. Rollo's confidence lives in his hands.

Ingrid's face wears the curve of a smile, and appears to glow with vitality's elusive ember. Rollo suspects she has stolen any remnants of color that may have belonged to him. He suspects perhaps this development is an attempt to wrest control of the fort. To wrest control of him. He imagines something once dormant in Ingrid meeting the perfect mixture of conditions in which to erupt, shifting every dynamic their foundation rests upon. The enormity of Rollo's weakness occupies him. He feels the hunger wrought by endless unfinished meals. He moves toward the discarded plates of the dinner past. His is piled with the unconsumed. Strength on a plate when it should be in him. Contrary to his plate, Ingrid's is empty, the contents have found a home within her, spreading strength throughout her body. He pulls his remaining sustenance close and fills his desperate mouth, feeling the food break into a fungal slush primed for entry. The unfamiliar intake travels downward, slowed by the narrowed passage of an emaciated esophagus. The intolerable quantity is cast out, landing back on the plate.

"Are you okay?"

There is no response forthcoming. Nothing to assuage Ingrid's curiosity. No means by which to achieve dignity. Rollo holds the plate close and tips the dreck back into his mouth, determined to keep it down this time. The bulk sits within puffed cheeks, pushing against his pursed lips. A small amount travels downward, slowly transferring the contents from mouth to stomach.

"I do not understand why you want to force it down. Why are you eating like that?"

Heavy breaths escape his stretched throat, emerging amidst wheezes and coughs. Rollo feels as though he has accomplished something. He is just not sure what. He knows Ingrid is staring. Her eyes direct columns of strange energy that settle in his skin, making it itch. Now, more than ever, he wishes he could understand the sound of her thoughts. The compulsion that led them to this point. The emergence of a new order.

"You seem distressed," she says. "Are you sure this is something you want to do?"

Each new question removes more of Rollo's subjectivity. He is not permitted to respond in the manner he would like. A thought passes through many filters before it emerges as something communicated. Each filter works to remove venom. Spite. Responsibility. Rollo's filters remove so much there is nothing left to communicate.

"I am fine. Just hungry. When do we start?"

Ingrid approaches Rollo. Arm outstretched. Fingers bent slightly at each joint. She presses the back of her hand into his forehead. Ingrid's touch. Her flesh merging briefly with his. This tactile interaction does not comprehend itself. The two have not touched one another for longer than can be measured. This absence of touch extends beyond time. The chill of her hand sinks into the sweating heat of his brow. Ingrid reads his heat, searching for signs of illness. Degradation of physical condition could compromise what they have agreed to do.

"I think you should go to bed early," she says. "I want you to start collecting materials tomorrow. If you are not feeling as well as you could, focus may elude you."

She places a hand on either shoulder and guides him to his feet. He finds he is allowing her to lead him toward his bed. Myriad mental voices form a chorus, repeating the thought: *this is not what I want*. The voices are ignored in favor of whatever force compels his acquiescence. Gentle pressure is applied to either shoulder. Ingrid communicating through her hands. Encouraging him to sit on the bed. Then to lie down. The touch of another is new to Rollo. It casts a hypnotic fog he struggles to see beyond. Her hands are removed. The current connecting him and her is severed, but the residual touch remains, ensuring continued pliancy. Ingrid's confident hands pick up a blanket and drape it over Rollo's pathetic form. Ensconcing him. Capturing the hypnotism, forcing it to remain active. *This is not what I want. This is not what I want. This is not what I want. This is not what I want.*

"I'm going to make sure you have food waiting for you when you wake."

Rollo's eyes are fixed ahead. Ingrid produces curious sounds beyond his line of sight. These are sounds that provoke something beyond what is remembered. Something a pre-fort version of him might have experienced. There is a thought, residing in theoretical realms, that Rollo once had parents. He must have been born to someone. The sounds Ingrid continues to produce are of a type one might associate with the notion of parents. Perhaps there was a point in Rollo's life where he lay frozen, similar to now. Where someone he might have called a mother or father made these sounds when he should have been asleep.

Rollo is going to be a parent.

The thought now feeds on this moment in time. He is experiencing something that the child… *his* child might experience. Bricolage music played on domesticity. Ingrid is rehearsing. Readying herself for her debut as a mother. Training innate functions pertaining to parenthood. Developing the fledgling form of new patterns. Patterns beyond Rollo. Patterns beyond the fort. He longs to learn these patterns alongside Ingrid. If a new pattern emerges beyond his understanding, he will fall behind. Loss and risk combine their dark strength and run circles around his mind. Distorting the moment and directing Rollo's body to shut down and introduce itself to the world of sleep.

His last waking thoughts take a merciful detour from Ingrid and the baby and visit the readings in the Cerebellum Chamber. There will be no readings tonight. The atmospheric properties of the fort will, for the first time, become a horrible unknown. His relationship with the surrounding environment is already changing. When time dictates the baby's arrival into their physical world, the dread will become much greater. Change is scheduled to arrive and there is no security measure Rollo can perform to deny it access.

Ingrid is at the bureau, notebook open. Her eyes smile at the impending existence of what she sees. Circle within circle within circle within circle…

6.

When Rollo considers the introduction of a baby to their dynamic, the fear it invokes is new and uncomfortable. Life within the fort entails a necessary fear, which functions as an added security measure. All fear, until now, has been used to keep their world safe from whatever exists outside. It is fear Rollo uses to keep himself moving forward. Now he begins to comprehend the existence of an anxiety quite different to what he has always known. A hive within is awakened. In this simple request, Ingrid cannot be denied. There will be a baby. There has to be a baby. Rollo senses the death of the absence he shares with Ingrid, a death that threatens to reignite blame between the two. The alteration of any dynamic is the death of that dynamic. Rollo and Ingrid were fueled by a dynamic based on distance, but the baby is pulling the two closer together, unconcerned by what may result.

In this development, Ingrid resides in the pit of Rollo's stomach, churning his anxiety into thick butter. His role in the baby's creation feels perfunctory. Just enough to satisfy the basic criteria in which the baby can be considered *theirs* rather than *hers*. The residual bewitchment of her hands has evaporated, yet he feels no more control over his agency. He moves against himself to satisfy her. In the task he has been given, he feels as though he is participating in his own end.

He must select the wool. The child must be the result of their combined efforts. Rollo will set aside the best materials, materials intended for maintenance, and he will give them to Ingrid. With these materials Ingrid will build their child. It takes significant effort for Rollo to approach the task with integrity. He fools himself into believing inferior materials are the best so as not to dishonor the fort. The process is slow, exacting. Each selection is a potential trap diverting Rollo's attention. All he can trust is pain. When a selection results in pain, he knows he has the best. He resents the child and resents his role in the creation of the child. He resents Ingrid for introducing the concept of the child. He resents Ingrid for her control over the process. The strength of his resentment resonates with shocking clarity. Immediate waves of guilt surround the wicked thoughts he is producing. The guilt pushes him further in a direction contrary to his desire. As resentment for the baby elevates, so does his commitment to the task of producing the baby. Thoughts of sabotage stoke guilt, which pulls him further away from agency. He becomes exactly what Ingrid needs him to be in response to not wanting to be what she wants.

...

The material stockpiles never seem enough. Each sits neatly according to type. Rollo will not allow for cross-contamination and should two different materials come into contact prior to their use, he has determined they must be destroyed. Each individual component is accorded this respect and subjected to a process that, to Rollo, is akin to sanctification. He grows troubled when he considers a baby constructed from such finery and wonders if perhaps a certain amount of imperfection is necessary. The qualities of any individual surely rest within the core of their imperfections. How can one be determined from the other without the impurity of idiosyncrasy? Could it be that perfection, in and of itself, is the ultimate failure? A place one should strive for, but never reach? Something beginning at the end can never truly begin. How can existence mean anything when lost to perfection?

Rollo is able to convince himself his child needs imperfection.

He controls the mounting guilt with something similar to logical reasoning and replaces a ball of wool with one of lesser quality. If their child is to truly embody them both, it must contain his imperfection. It must experience the weakness Rollo introduces to the bloodline. His staunch adherence to the needs of the fort could be construed as a weakness. Preventing the child access to the best materials the fort has to offer is Rollo's way of honoring the child. Surely Ingrid will introduce inconsistencies into the child when she uses her own imperfect hands to make it. Each defect will be Ingrid's way of honoring the child with her own imperfection. Rollo has a duty to do the same.

...

Pathogenic air gains strength from its dormancy. Expanding. Breaking through what binds it. Imperfection, abundant and strong, peels apart the pathogenic shell. Permitting infection of the stable air. The disease in all things will find a way to thrive. It possesses patience quite unfathomable to conscious experience.

Pathogenic Bildungsroman

He alone was bacterium, existing on the polished floor of an empty stage. Absorbed in the loneliness of his reflection. In want of progeny in which to share the expanse of stage. He alone was bacterium, seeking materials in impossible places. Materials were food and property. Food so it may grow. Property so it may understand what ownership meant.

As one alone, bacterium enjoyed the food, taking it inside, introducing it to him. Within him was finite space. Growth bound to limitation that, when reached, introduced bacterium to its fission. To bacterium, binary fission came disguised as death. Tearing him apart. Leaving him both less and more.

He alone was bacterium, waking from death, staring into the heart of stage lights. At once seeing everything and nothing. Not yet aware that he was no longer alone in his loneliness.

He alone was new bacterium, prone beside old bacterium. Unaware that one came from the other. The two bacteria wandered the expanse of empty stage. Each seeking more food, more property, and gorging upon what was found.

Both bacteria experienced a new process of fission. Both believed they would die. Both unaware they were instead conducting the introduction of further life. Each bacteria woke as one of four. Abidance to their pattern soon ensures each bacterium wakes as one of eight. Then 16. Then 32.

Without intervention, materials in which each bacterium can feed remain abundant. With abundance comes continuation of process and multiplication of their population.

A society of bacteria exists on a crowded stage, rehearsing lines fed by the inspiration of pattern. Now at want of an audience in which to experience performance. The performance is further fission. The performance is perpetuation of existence. A drive toward multiplication.

The audience sought is merely environment. The audience is space in which to thrive. A host willing to provide materials. Food and property. Food and property. Greater numbers of bacteria require more. More. More. More. More. More.

What of the first Bacterium? The bacterium to which the society owes so much. It exists as one of its innumerable facsimiles, no longer aware it was first. This is not a society allowing for thought to grow in isolation. The process is thought. The bacteria are signals dictated by process.

The successful proliferation of bacteria will eventually destroy the stage on which it lives. The process only knows growth, and growth can only work toward its end.

7.

The outline of a humanoid form has been sketched on graph paper by Ingrid's hand. The empty space inside the outline represents her baby. Possibility exists in abundance, almost overwhelming in what it offers. So many directions. No way of knowing if one direction is preferable to another. A dilemma pulls into focus. How can one create a child that possesses both the certainty of choice and the unpredictability of chance? Ingrid feels chance must dictate some portion of the endeavor.

She scrawls chaotic shapes over the outline, obscuring what it once was. Her child will not be the result of a blueprint; rather her hands will move as their immediate will dictates, knitting something potentially flawed, but undeniably unique. The eradicated outline provokes relief. The agony of choice diminishes into the momentum of process. A process of automated creation. Elements of the child must remain a mystery. Misunderstood. Poorly translated. Everyone, living or otherwise, is entitled to secrets. It is within the darkness of our secrets that personality is born. What we conceal resides at the core of who we are.

The materials collected by Rollo sit in neat, separated piles, calling out for veneration. Ingrid squeezes her eyes shut and reaches into the collection of material. She extracts the first item. A ball of light green yarn. It is a system contingent on the memory of tactility. The ghosts of former touch translating all touch that follows. Ingrid's hands work in accordance to a history hidden from the conscious.

Light green yarn is extracted, therefore their child will be light green. Reason gathers around Ingrid, attempting to dissuade her from such a system, but she perseveres. Each blind excursion into the material threatens internal anarchy. Each choice undermined by lack of choice.

Ingrid stares at her knitting needles, somehow understanding that they possess a tension of three millimeters. A glossary of knitting-specific abbreviations, hidden until now, sparks synapses.

Alt, approx., beg, bet, BO, CA, CB, CC, cdd, ch, cm, cn, CO, cont, cross 2 L, cross 2 R, dc, dec, DK, dpn, EON, EOR, FC, fl, foll, g, g st, grp, hdc, hk, in, inc, incl, k, k tbl, k-b, k-wise, kfb, k2tog, k2tog tbl, kll, krl, LC, LH, lp, LT, m, M1, M1A, M1L, M1R, M1T, MB, mc, mm, no, oz, p, p tbl, p-b, p-wise, p2tog, p2tog tbl, pat, pm, pnso, pop, prev, psso, pu, RC, rem, rep, rev St st, RH, rib, rnd, RS, RT, sc, sk, sk2p, SKP, sl, sl st, sl1, slik, sl1p, sps, ss, ssk, ssp, sssk, st, St st, tbl, tog, won, wrn, WS, wyib, wyif, yb, yd, yfon, yfrn, yfwd, yo, yo2, yon, yrn.

These all mean something to her. Each can be decoded and acted upon. Knitting is a language Ingrid understands; it is only now that she discovers she understands. Ingrid's mind is flooded with a burst of memory, too voluminous to parse. It can only be experienced in separation from the drive to know detail.

Ingrid cannot locate the origin of the memory. Like anything born of an apparent nowhere, it is assumed the 'nowhere' is a fallacy. Something indicative of possible discoveries to come. The needles are held with certainty. She performs something she understands to be 'casting on' with a technique she understands to be the 'thumb method.' With the light green yarn fastened to the needle, she casts stitch after stitch, covering the needle's length. The unencumbered needle joins its partner and begins picking at the stitches, working its way into a loop. The method continues. Rows are formed. Slow commencement becomes steady adherence to an understood pattern of movement. Cognition relinquishes control to the unfolding pattern.

Ingrid allows the process to push her aside, content to witness the fluidity of her movement and dazzle at her ability. Ingrid's pattern is the womb in which their child is forming.

...

Rollo is denied access to the Prefrontal Chamber while Ingrid knits. Without her consent, he decides to watch through the security mirrors of the Occipital Chamber. Her reflection is diluted as it passes from mirror to mirror, eventually arriving as a barely distinct shape before Rollo's eyes. He can tell she is seated and her arms are lost in activity, but the important information found in the clarity of detail is absent.

Rollo has been told a gestation period is in progress. Something that must occur privately between mother and child. The father's presence can have no place here. While knitting is performed, access to the Prefrontal Chamber is restricted. The knitting seems ceaseless. Rollo is unable to determine time passed or progress made. He leaves the Occipital Chamber and lingers just beyond the Prefrontal Chamber's entrance, listening to the rhythmic click of excited needles. His proximity to the restricted area inspires feelings of guilt.

When Ingrid becomes aware of Rollo near the entrance, she ushers him away. Forbidding his return until dinner, where their child in progress is locked in the bureau drawer. He knows he owns the strength to force the drawer open, but something intangible prevents this action. A role has been assigned and is abided by for no other reason than the existence of the role. He makes a point of not looking toward the drawer, projecting an aura of distraction, as if his thoughts reside with maintenance rather than his diminishing importance. Truth does not align with his faux-distraction. Maintenance is falling behind. Daily tasks no longer occur daily. Infrequency becomes a normative state.

He thinks of nothing but the baby. As the construction

process evolves, greater levels of intensity are directed toward the thought. When the two sit to eat, Rollo is full of questions without voice. Ingrid is full of unavailable answers. His baby in progress resides so close. It would not require exertion to reach over and touch the bureau. He can feel the polished surface of the drawer. The intricate brass of the handle. The waft of enclosed scent escaping as the drawer slides open. The assemblage of wool, day-by-day becomes his progeny. Strands binding together, becoming more than themselves.

Ingrid's hands are not Rollo's hands. Ingrid's hands orchestrate creation's performance. Without maintenance, Rollo's hands do not feel like Rollo's hands. Rollo's hands belong with the baby. Rollo's hands could produce a baby too. It would likely be of higher quality than what Ingrid's hands are capable of. To what use does she put her hands? Little more than dormant flesh in the world of work. Her fingers belong around a pencil, guiding the production of words. Rollo is a builder. Rollo has aptitude in his hands. They understand the patterns of construction. The language of production. Perhaps if the child could be built with words Ingrid would be most suitable. This process of baby construction is no different to refilling a pillow.

…

Discontent continues to mount. Rollo feels he would have finished the baby by now. Confining himself to the Occipital Chamber he continues his vigil. Clarity refuses. There is nothing he can see but a shape representing Ingrid. The dominant feeling is exclusion, of which the baby has become a symbol. A baby that exists as little more than concept. His resentment struggles to find a comfortable destination. At one moment it sits with Ingrid and another, with the baby. Anything resembling the life he had enjoyed prior to the baby concept has lost strength and fallen victim to replacement thoughts wearing dread. Rollo no longer feels the significance of insignificance the daily patterns once instilled. Without the meditation of pattern, Rollo has nothing.

...

"What gender will the baby be?"

Rollo has been building to this question. Of all the questions left unasked, this one fought hardest for his voice. The affectless delivery belies its importance. A gender cannot be attributed without his influence. He cannot allow it.

"I don't know."

Ingrid shifts in her seat, placing a protective hand on the bureau. Asking the question introduces a sense of danger.

"You must know. You are building it."

Rollo pushes the point, elevating the danger. Ingrid moves her chair, obscuring the bureau completely, denying Rollo a potential line of sight.

"I really do not know. It is not up to you or I to decide the gender of our baby."

It does not make sense. Rollo's belly rumbles in response to the inexplicable answer. Ingrid is denying the existence of her agency. Suggesting something beyond her influence will determine gender.

"I want a girl," says Rollo.

Ingrid assaults Rollo with her gaze, flooding him with violent mentality. She pours her will into it. Giving everything she has to the task. Rollo acts in direct opposition, tempting her focus to falter. Manipulating her away from the bureau and taking the baby. Finishing the baby. Forcing a gender of his choosing upon it.

"We might have a girl. We might have a boy. It is not up to you or I to decide."

The whistling sound of Rollo's thought increases in pitch and volume. Ingrid counters, attacking him with psychic babble.

...

The entrance to the Prefrontal Chamber has been sewn shut. Until Ingrid has finished the baby, Rollo is not permitted access, even to eat and sleep. She has covered the mirror that allows visual access from the Occipital Chamber. He has been told access will be reinstated when the baby is ready. Time, an ambiguous notion at best in the context of the fort, seems to cease its passage. Rollo's exclusion finds stasis.

Ingrid keeps one eye on the entrance and the other eye on her work. The baby now exists as several components. Two legs of slightly differing lengths sit plump with stuffing. Two arms are about to undergo the same process. The torso awaits its limbs. Off to the side sits their child's head. Rudimentary features illustrate its face. A line of black yarn for the mouth. Straight. No applicable emotion. Two red circles of yarn for eyes. Subtly raised eyebrows suggesting the moment prior to surprise. Another straight line. Vertical. A slight curve at the base. This is the nose. Clustered yellow strands have become hair. The head will wait until all other elements have become one.

She would like to dedicate more time to the assembly, but fears Rollo will not allow this. She knows something about the baby Rollo does not and feels it will displease him. Contrary to Rollo's desires, the baby is a boy. He will think Ingrid is responsible. It is only by virtue of her hands this is true. Cognition played no role in the gender. She is convinced of it. There was no awareness of the developing male characteristics until after the characteristics emerged.

Ingrid senses, at some level, she knew their child would be a boy. She feels greater kinship with the male experience, but does not know why. Some things are just known as so. If forces beyond her deigned it appropriate she should influence its gender somehow, in what way could she be blamed? The wool in Ingrid's hands is more than wool. The baby exists beyond a collection of sewn shapes. The baby existed before Ingrid existed.

The determination of what has become is of a chain extending further back and farther forward than time conceives.

This, like anything, can be calculated as so. This is more than Rollo. This is more than Ingrid. This is more than the fort.

8.

The readings suggest universal change in atmosphere. Numbers congress in unfamiliar order. Rollo examines readings past, searching for precedents. It becomes apparent the numbers have found a new order. One beyond Rollo's capacity to calculate and comprehend. It cannot be determined whether such an order represents jeopardy. Rollo is unable to dismiss the notion of the baby as pathogen, infecting the fort's bloodstream. A movement toward slow death. His journey through past readings stretches back, detailing the evolution of understanding. Early readings are incomplete. Tentative in penmanship. Rollo conjures an earlier version of himself, overwhelmed by data. Unsure how to document the deluge. At a loss to decipher what they wish to convey. Numbers are crossed out. Re-written. Doubled over. At want for comprehension. Wilting beneath the power of his ignorance.

    The development of aptitude often defies perception. It exists in steps, the ascent of which can only be viewed from a detached distance. The transition from step-to-step rarely feels like transition at all; it is like a rectilinear continuation. One assumed trapped within shiftless stagnation. It is here most will forfeit a pursuit. Too many incorrect notes distract from the increased instance of correct notes. It is only when one is prepared to experience failure, to bury themselves in the heart of its heart, that achievement can be found. It is only with the detachment of time's passage that ascent reveals itself.

    In the history of his readings, Rollo becomes aware of aptitude's path. The rise of true confidence unattached to the façades erected by ego. He taught himself to understand numbers by force of will. These new numbers seem to mock his aptitude. Any translation appears lost as those attempted in his early records. Nothing he already knows is applicable to now. Ingrid and the baby have knocked his focus off-balance, rendering the required will impossible.

Rollo is immured in the non-Prefrontal Chambers, forbidden access to that which he wants most. This is the reality in which he broods. He remains with the indecipherable readings in the Cerebellum Chamber, forgoing food and water as though this forced decrepitude will punish Ingrid. The slowly ticking numbers are obsessed over. As obsession increases and ignorance screams, the less the numbers mean. Inquiry is replaced with projected outcomes of foreboding. Lack of understanding is a blank canvas on which to paint paranoia. Everything unknown is danger and harm.

He vacillates between directing his resentment toward Ingrid, then the baby. As the pendulum directs blame at one, he feels great sympathy for the other, until the swing shifts and attitudes are reversed. In one reality the baby is an innocent tool used by Ingrid to manipulate the fort's dynamic. In another, Ingrid is the tool, being used as a conduit for an external malevolence in the baby's form.

Logic attempts to steer Rollo toward reason and probability. Probability suggests neither Ingrid nor the baby intend harm upon him or the fort. It is natural for one to seek the continuation of life, the advent of legacy. Were it not for the drive exemplified by Ingrid, life could not continue. How can one place blame on a baby for existing? These logical tangents only add guilt to Rollo's mounting paranoia. The logic is not powerful enough to vanquish the paranoia. The two dance about Rollo's skull, one gaining the upper hand before losing it to the other.

He stares at the numbers. Through the numbers. Waiting and conflict define him.

...

Ingrid need only attach the head and her baby is complete. A sense of peace prevents the execution of this final step. When the head is sewn into place, the baby is born and Rollo must be permitted access. Ingrid feels compelled to protect the baby from all potential harm, which, to her horror, includes Rollo. She assumes this is maternal instinct, which is a reasonable protective mechanism, but the guilt refuses to diminish. Rollo would never cause her baby harm. She knows this. It is his baby too. Any involvement he enforces upon the process is the result of love. Of excitement.

Her hands glow with the vitality of creation. The nearly formed expression of life exists as a testament to what she is capable of. Who she is. What she can achieve beyond Rollo's intervention.

She holds the unattached head aloft, rotating it slowly in her hand. Experiencing its existence. Her eyes drink in the details to ensure an intimate understanding unlike any other. This is Ingrid's son. A manifestation of her. She brings the woolen head toward her face and rubs it against her beard. The head longs for attachment to its body. Ingrid longs for this attachment too and knows it cannot be delayed. Life wants what it wants and she is in no position to control that.

Thread pinched between excited fingers. Needle accepts thread without complaint. Thread tied to needle. Body in wait. Head in wait. Ingrid in wait. Head positioned above body in ghostly detachment. Brought closer. Head kisses body. Body kisses head. Ingrid bows and kisses both. The weaving needle trails the thread, binding via its passage. Ingrid sews tight stitches. Stitch sitting against stitch sitting against stitch. The crowd of ordered stitches form a strengthening bond. Space between each stitch must be eradicated. Thread is pulled. Head tightens. Straightens. Joining the body in greater unity with each needle weave. Her breath trails thin wisps of carbon dioxide from pursed lips lost in concentration. A circle of stitches destined to meet, heralding new life. Circle formed. Thread sits against thread. Between the kiss of Ingrid's thumb and pointer emerges the needle. The trail of thread is severed with Ingrid's gentle teeth. Two lengths of thread now exist. One length encircles the spool. The other is frozen in the stitching's complex path. The spool is placed aside. The thread sprouting from the stitching's complexity is tied off. Baby is born.

Joyful tears climb Ingrid. Each seeks their passage out. Manifesting as irritation in the eyes before finding their escape and traveling downward. Exploring the length of her nose and dripping like kisses upon the newborn. Ingrid shakes with emotion. Desperate to cradle the baby in crossed arms, but terrified of causing harm. Instead she brushes her fingers over its innocent face. The texture of the wool in this moment will never be forgotten. Lowered lips press down on its belly. Her ear replaces the lips and listens to imagined heartbeats. Through jittering seizures of excitement, Ingrid's hands lift the new life.

Ingrid supports the baby's weight and draws it toward her, pressing it into her chest, feeding it with her heartbeat. Understanding her life is bound by this new addition, too overwhelming to describe. This moment exists for no one but the two. Rollo cannot be introduced yet. He must remain outside of this experience until the baby understands Ingrid as his mother. There is too much Ingrid wants to feel before outsiders are permitted to interfere. Since the idea of the baby found form within her, the moment of birth is one Ingrid has afforded a great deal of importance to. Significance can be difficult to experience, and when one does, it must be held in place and experienced fully.

...

The numbers are ticking in frenzied insect clicks. Rollo snaps away from his abjection and watches the display. His heart quickens to match the barrage of clicks and feeds his body with panic. A final change has occurred. A change too powerful for the numbers to translate. Rollo knows the chaos of these numbers means the baby has arrived. Why has he not been told? What properties of the fort have altered to accommodate this new addition? How does it know?

…

The darkness of this night belongs to Ingrid and her child. In the limbo between wake and sleep, she melts into the bed. The baby rests facedown on her chest, moving up and down in tandem with the slow breath of contentment. Sleep does not have a place in this moment. Not for Ingrid. This is the first night between the two and it must be experienced. Remembered. Drawn out in caramel trails that refuse to break.

"I am your mother. You are my child. We are separate but we are one. I beat the heart you cannot. I see that which your eyes cannot. I hear your voice where no sound exists. I hear what you long to hear. I pass what you need through my body and give it to you in untold abundance. You are the enormity of me. The enormity that alone, I cannot be. Thank you for being. Thank you for allowing my hand to guide yours."

She fights the sleep that arrives, understanding the fight cannot last. Understanding she is now sleeping for him.

Rollo can hear the shifting texture of Ingrid's thoughts. New characteristics and shapes. He focuses his attention toward them. Wishing he could comprehend them. Shake them from their wordlessness. Isolation knows its own character as such, and reminds the isolated of that character with every movement of mind.

"The baby does not belong to you. The baby belongs to the baby. We are here to protect the baby. Guide the baby. Do not keep it from me. Allow me to feel what you feel in this moment. Allow the baby to know me. To understand I mean it no harm. Please let me in. Please let me in. You cannot do this."

9.

"There is someone you need to meet."

Ingrid appears calm, standing over Rollo slumped before the numbers. Sleep has remained outside of possibility, floating in a mass everywhere but inside. His glazed eyes consider Ingrid's presence, working to process the visual information and feed it toward floundering comprehension. Her persistent form feeds neurons, assembling sense data.

Rollo's awareness of Ingrid in the flesh disassembles elements of paranoia that have been attacking him. He knows why she stands before him.

"The baby?"

"Yes. He is ready."

The 'he' pronoun is absorbed. Gender has been decided in direct opposition to Rollo's desire. Their baby should be a she. A son makes very little sense, contradicting a natural inclination he cannot parse. He feels compelled to label it a 'she.' He wonders if such an act may confuse the child's identity. Blame forms in a growing stockpile he will direct at Ingrid when its power is sufficient.

"Take me to it."

Ingrid turns to leave, waiting for Rollo to stand. The asymmetric position of his body draped before the computer's numbers have stretched his ligaments and tendons to match the position. The nerves in Rollo's back send pain signals throughout his body, stiffening the muscles, slowing movement. Joints crack as he moves toward Ingrid who, without looking, begins the journey toward the Prefrontal Chamber. Each of Rollo's steps produces a pop, audible enough for Ingrid to hear. She turns and commands quiet with a finger against her lips.

"He is sleeping."

Rollo sends signals to the pain, imploring it to lose its volume. It shifts in response and floods the joints with heat, loosening and soothing. His introduction to the baby cannot disturb it. Ingrid has already formed an initial bond. A bond deprived of Rollo, who is nothing more than a stranger. An interloper seeking to disrupt a recently born dynamic.

...

The Prefrontal Chamber is caliginous, searching for illumination it cannot find. Waning moss glow is fading. Silhouettes are dying.

"I cannot see. Why is there no light?"

Rollo shuffles forward with outstretched arms searching for obstructions to avoid.

"The baby is sleeping. It needs the dark to sleep."

He stumbles into a chair and lowers himself down to escape the directionless sense of falling.

"I want to see the baby."

The sound of Ingrid's movements suggest ease. Her feet move forward without hesitation somewhere toward the middle of the chamber.

"Follow my voice. I am with the baby."

Her voice is a malicious whisper trying to set the example she wishes Rollo's voice to follow. Rollo falls forward, his knees finding the ground. He crawls toward the whisper.

"Where are you?"

"Over here."

His direction alters slightly and he continues to crawl. It seems he should have reached her by now. Distance is mocking him. Before he opens his mouth again to seek guidance, he feels a warm hand clasp his wrist. The sensation startles him. He inhales breaths intended to calm, but cannot find the volume of oxygen his lungs require.

"Stay still. He is right here."

Rollo motions to reach toward the 'here,' but Ingrid's hand prevents this desire finding form.

"I want to feel the baby."

"You cannot see. You might hurt it. Wait until later."

Being denied access to something sitting so close troubles Rollo. He is being asked to accept the baby's existence on faith. Faith is anathema in his world of numbers and precaution. No empirical evidence pertaining to the baby has been brought forward. There is nothing to scrutinize, therefore there may be nothing. This possibility is considered until nothing suggests nothing. If their baby is nonexistent, what has Ingrid been doing here?

"You must allow me to verify the baby."

Ingrid's hand applies more pressure to Rollo's wrist.

"When it has finished sleeping you may see it. You may hold it. Until then you must trust that it is here sleeping. Just as I have said."

"Can I talk to it? Will you permit it access to my voice?"

In the silence that follows, Rollo's ears search for sounds signaling the presence of another. His ears are not trained to hear what he needs them to hear. Beyond the escalating chatter of Ingrid's tumbling thoughts, he hears nothing.

"You may talk to him, but you must whisper."

...

Ingrid is hiding the truth. In the time before collecting Rollo, she hid the baby in the Frontal Chamber. A place she knows Rollo will not visit. Following their first night together as mother and son, a protective urgency instilled itself. Until Rollo's attitude and demeanor around the baby is understood, he poses a risk to the child's safety. Whether this risk is deliberate or the result of inexperience she cannot say. She hopes for the latter but lives in fear of the former. The child exists through her and she through it. Harm to one is harm to the other. Too much is at stake to allow precaution not to take precedence. In Rollo she lacks knowledge. He exists in the form of something recognizable, but nothing understood.

Ingrid understands her role in terms that diminish guilt. While hiding the baby there were only thoughts of right. The continuation of deceit is a continuation of protection. She knows the Frontal Chamber will be kind to the baby. Its walls know only the meaning of Ingrid, which is a meaning that nurtures the baby. Nestled among the secret letters, the baby is free to absorb Ingrid's most personal terrain. The letters are a directory of psyche that will work toward teaching the baby what it means to experience life. She understands the baby does not possess life in a typical manner. It is incapable of thought so must be fed by Ingrid's. These written thoughts will instill Ingrid's bias in the child, and this will extend to perceptions of Rollo. It is unavoidable. She reasons that a child will absorb their parents' bias regardless of any attempts to keep it from them. Perhaps the poor masking of latent bias is more detrimental. Parents' words saying one thing and their eyes saying another. Confusion inspired by dishonesty yet conducted with honest intentions. Hiding the truth amplifies the truth, eventually drowning out the lies expressed in honor of the truth. A child should never learn their parents' truth via their parents' dishonesty.

Ingrid was comfortable sharing her truth with her child. In preventing Rollo immediate access to the child, the child would know, as Ingrid knows, that Rollo is not someone in which trust can be placed. Rollo must earn his child. He must prove himself and show he is comfortable with his role in the new dynamic. The child is not another fort for Rollo to control.

There is a suspicion growing inside Ingrid the materials selected by Rollo for the baby's construction were not of uniform quality. Evidence supporting this suspicion is absent, but the feeling is there. When Ingrid's hands caress the woolen surface of the baby's skin, her tactility weeps. While this uneasy phenomenon occurs, Rollo cannot be regarded as anything other than dangerous.

...

Ingrid asks Rollo to stay out of the Prefrontal Chamber for a few more nights. He believes there is nothing to stay away from. His words were delivered to his supposed child, but it did not feel as though his words were heard in any sense. The words themselves, poorly chosen, conveyed nothing and have already been forgotten. This was not the introduction Rollo desired. He begins to hope the baby is a lie and, with the shift in desire, begins to feel it is not. That it lay before him the whole time, unmoved by its father's voice. The fastest way to make something so is to wish it were not.

He leaves the Prefrontal Chamber as requested, not so much for Ingrid or the baby, but for himself. His troubled mind struggles to breathe in the chamber's darkness. The moss has ebbed to nothing. His eyes have found nothing and strain with unsuccessful mydriasis. For the first time in memory, he wishes to escape the absence of light that, until now, he found great comfort in.

"When can I see the baby?"

He asks this question as obligation, still unsure there is anything to see.

"When I come for you next, bring more moss."

Ingrid guides him out, pulling the blanket behind her, separating him from them. He feels a rush of ventilated air travel down the Medulla Shaft. The sensation relieves him. Light that once appeared dim now forces his eyes to squint in its perceived brightness. Time is spent observing the reality of his body. Understanding that in the presence of illumination it appears. Within the darkness of the Prefrontal Chamber, Rollo felt his erasure.

He moves to the Occipital Chamber, which appears brighter still, and gorges on the luminescent moss, burying his face within its damp softness, pressing his eyes into the light's heart. It is torn into mush by famished teeth and sucked down in wads, satisfying both hunger and thirst. Sleep's elusive cloud finds Rollo, covering him in its promise. He feels it envelop him, stealing the day. In a single breath, he slips quietly away, granted fleeting respite from the waking world of nightmares.

10.

Entry into an empty stomach. Food becomes bolus, which the body steals from. Saliva steals starch. Agitated acid steals protein. Bolus becomes chyme. Thick food product. Ravaged by the body's need. Chyme continues beyond the stomach. Food becomes a contortion disconnected from its origin. It is dissected. Deconstructed. Parts within parts. What once grew, a life unto itself, is absorbed into the blood. Picked at. What is deemed unnecessary is discarded. Treated as waste. Expelled. The body remembers every process. The food becomes a part of the body's memory. It travels the blood until it fades away. Everything individual is temporal. The chain of transitory process never ends. One will always find another. Life is process.

Rollo leeches strength from food and sleep. His body performs integral acts of maintenance. He wakes into something different. Events prior to sleep have separated from the emotion, offering clarity. Different emotions have introduced themselves. These new emotions shift Rollo's perspective. The arrival of a new perspective lends credence to that perspective by virtue of being new. Old perspective has had time to digest in the mind's stomach no longer causing upset. That which satisfies the mind's hunger is always afforded greater attention.

Aided by the vitality of sustenance and rest, Rollo regrets his capitulation to Ingrid. It happened too easily. Access to his child has been denied. Their dynamic subsists on absence of communication, yet he allowed her words to dictate his actions. In his world of maintenance, life is action. The fort is predicated on his drive to act. The baby's introduction concerns the fort and is therefore within Rollo's purview. If Ingrid will not allow Rollo to engage with the baby, he will merely disregard that which Ingrid disallows. Whether permission is granted or not, he will come to know the baby.

He will try and talk his way to the baby before applying physicality. Use the words that now seem to exist between them. Should his words fail to find receptive ears, he will push Ingrid aside. If such overt action results in distress or anger, he will endure it. Anything can be endured. All one need do is wait. Emotions are short-lived creatures, quick to drop their essence like a cloud drops rain.

In the Occipital Chamber he pulls away a section of luminescent moss, wrapping it gently in a cloth, which dulls and preserves its glow. A smaller section is pulled away which he eats, allowing his body to experience the mental and physical strength it provides. The moss sits comfortably inside, breaking down without complaint. In the Sylvian Fissure he washes. The water is weaker than before. Less inclined. It drips rather than flows. Like a tear one tries to prevent. He moves the pathetic wet around his body, feeling it evaporate beneath the heat of his hand. The occasional cough of grey water douses him, before the pathetic dripping continues. His skin only relinquishes its filth with persistence. Trapped grime bleeds from his body, washing away, dying in water traps.

...

Ingrid is compelled toward an action she is unable to reconcile. There is an addition to her son she longs to make. A conscious addition contrary to the principal of natural development she has tried to abide by. Within this compulsion is a sense her son is not yet complete. As though whatever existence it possesses is a step away from true existence. Time is spent focusing on this addition. Rationalizing it. Building reconciliation between what she wants and what she deems right. Rationalization works to marry one extreme with the other, shaving off edges. Pushing toward the middle. Finding common ground where none has reason to exist. With commitment, anything can be correct.

Ingrid is able to find the reconciliation she desires via Rollo. When she has completed the final addition, Rollo will be able to interact with his son. This is a commitment she makes with discretion, trying to mask the commitment from her deeper self who understands the lie. The commitment rests on a precise course of action Rollo, although not aware of it, must abide by. Her commitment allows for its own retraction should Rollo deviate from the highly specific path she has built for him to follow. It is a path so complex not even Ingrid comprehends it. One she hopes Rollo will fail to follow. The commitment is designed to rationalize the baby's addition, and in that aim, it is successful.

Ingrid's son is moved to the Frontal Chamber. Into light. He is placed on his back, staring up at folds in the ceiling, taking in nothing. Taking in every detail. A needle's eye is introduced to red thread. The baby's belly juts outward, waiting for the needle's kiss. Ingrid's hand swoops toward the belly. The needle slides easily inside the child, who continues his entranced stare. Sewing's dance begins with caution. An unfamiliar pattern is expected. Ingrid's hand will guide the pattern into knowing. Stitching finds rhythm. Rhythm grants pace. A shape is forming on the child's new belly.

A red circle.

The circle concludes. Ingrid places the needle within its parameter and begins the rhythm once more. A slight change. The circle is smaller. The larger circle must accommodate it, but only just. The new circle must allow for a smaller circle to sit within it.

A red circle within a red circle.

Another circle begins to form within the second, becoming a third. Ingrid maintains a focus beyond her. A careful hand amplifies with greater care. Precision becomes more important and more difficult to achieve as the circles decrease in size.

A red circle within a red circle within a red circle.

Ingrid continues her task, attaching increasing importance to each new circle. The smaller the circle, the longer it takes, as the intricacy and care required intensify. The baby remains still, ever patient. Allowing the addition to its body. Understanding, via Ingrid's understanding, this needs to happen. Its belly absorbs the concentric circles into its identity.

Ingrid has decided the circles will be her son's name. A name that fights verbalization, but a name that encapsulates everything a name seeks. In their world of unuttered names, a name should rise above its spoken form, becoming more than speaking allows. It is tailored to their fort world. It clings to its belly. Always transmitting identity. Distinguishing it from all else unlike any name before it. The memory of thread sewn with care speaks beyond the merely spoken. Perhaps if Ingrid possessed such a name, it would still have a purpose. It would mean something beyond the pragmatic need to label one thus when placed against the other. In this thought, Ingrid resents her name. Unlike Rollo, she will never forget her name. She will never forget his name. Perhaps beyond the pragmatism of labeling, all names mean something.

Her son sits complete. A part of their world. Informing all to come in whatever capacity that might entail. Ingrid picks up the baby and stares into the detail of her handiwork. The circles are imperfect, which in itself possesses its own perfection. Gentle hands under each plush arm pull the baby toward Ingrid's face. The raised belly circles meet her forehead, tarnished with the sweat of concentration. A circuit forms between mother and son that will never break. Energy is born that powers the connection.

...

Rollo lurks at the Prefrontal Chamber's entrance, training his ear to interpret sound. He is unaware Ingrid and his baby have moved to the Frontal Chamber, rendering his aural vigil redundant. His ears invent non-existent sound, which his brain processes as real. A rush of air from a distant vent becomes a threnody dedicated to Rollo's isolation and want. It is the imagined voice of Ingrid poisoning his child against him with hateful words devoid of truth. The resonance of wastewater drip is the baby responding to Ingrid's ventilation words. Nothing abides by his need.

He must enter the Prefrontal Chamber and confront the realities he invents. Regardless of his mental dissuasions, Rollo must know his child. He picks at the thread securing the sheet separating him from the chamber. The air that escapes does so with desperation. Stale air, trapped and longing to mix with fresh air beyond the chamber. This is what Ingrid has been taking into her body. This is the baby's reality. He tears away at the rest of the sheet, forcing the stitching apart. Stale oxygen floods and engulfs Rollo who keeps his mouth shut, not wanting to breathe whatever spite Ingrid has forced upon it. The Prefrontal Chamber sucks at the outside, giving itself back to the fort's bloodstream where it can flow with freedom.

The Chamber has lost all light. Faint tendrils of illumination reach from outside, but find quick death in the totality of the darkness. Rollo unwraps the moss collected from the Occipital Chamber and allows its light out, throwing itself upon every surface, lending it familiarity. His eyes navigate the newly revealed space around him, seeking out Ingrid. Attempting to understand. The cots are empty, as are the chairs. No one is there. Rollo's search transitions from careful to frantic. The power of absence overwhelms him. He would rather feel Ingrid's spite than the enormity of such loneliness.

11.

The body speaks the mind. Converting thought to physical language. Always betraying what we fear to speak. Eyes divert when lies occupy us. A hand obscures the face when fear overwhelms. We stare at unspoken objects. Nothing is hidden, only ignored. Our protection consists of another's self-obsession. When lost in themselves, another will never see you, whether you seek their gaze or not. Should one attract another's gaze, know that the language of your body is easily understood. Bodies communicate beyond the imperfection of words, occupying a language unbound to form. We understand the body of another because we understand our own.

Ingrid hears the frenzied sounds of Rollo's search, knowing she possesses the object he wishes to find. Furniture toppling and clamoring crockery. Peace disturbed by growing desperation. Both her son and the Frontal Chamber must be protected. Rollo is lost to a primal drive that demands his son. If she remains in the Frontal Chamber, she may be discovered, along with the importance she bestows upon the chamber. If she leaves the baby in the chamber and confronts Rollo, his search will grow more frenzied. It feels as though little choice remains outside of taking the baby to Rollo.

She carefully lifts her child and slides him beneath her shirt, allowing it some semblance of safety, however illusory. Its woolen skin presses against the skin of Ingrid's belly, creating the slightest itch. Almost imperceptible. An itch that longs to grow rather than lose itself beneath scratching fingernails.

The Frontal Chamber is left behind them. Ingrid moves

toward Rollo, one hand holding her son against the security offered by belly and shirt. The other is clenched into a fist so tight it consumes her fingers. This fist is unconscious in its manifestation and serves only to offer a place in which to store the growing fear. The veins in her hand swell with trapped blood denied passage to whitening fingers. She stares at the sheet torn away from the Prefrontal Chamber's entry.

Ingrid has underestimated Rollo. She predicted a turn of events that failed to eventuate, allowing Rollo to exert himself. He asserted his desire in a way defying precedent, wavering from his own pattern. Moving without Ingrid's understanding into a new pattern. This unknown pattern represents danger. In Ingrid's mind, if he is capable of forcing entry into the chamber, he is capable of feeding Ingrid imperfect materials in which to build the baby. Her conviction grows. Her paranoia has been justified beyond reasonable doubt. Rollo is capable of terrible things.

Rollo, more than before, must be kept from the baby.

In the new air of the Medulla Chamber, Ingrid is forced into spontaneity. The sound of Rollo's calamitous search maintains its urgency. While he remains convinced Ingrid and the baby are in the Prefrontal Chamber, Ingrid has an opportunity to seek safety. It seems unlikely that Rollo's Prefrontal search will last much longer. He will eventually reach the conclusion he is alone and broaden his efforts.

Although the Frontal Chamber calls to Ingrid, offering sanctuary to her and the baby, it is a risk she will not take. Should Rollo's search find them there, a great deal more will be lost. A part of Ingrid lives within that chamber and now, a part of her son too. It is a manifestation of their heart. In the absence of a biological childbirth, it is the organ they share. It represents the necessary separation of Ingrid and Rollo and the coming together of Ingrid and son. It is a place where separation finds strength in its voice, allowing for the development of her own possible truth.

She moves toward the Central Sulcus Emergency Tunnel. It is an obvious place to hide, somewhere Rollo will know to look, but her position will be temporary. Here she will formulate a plan. Although unspoken, it is understood the fort belongs to Rollo. While Ingrid spends her time sneaking between the Frontal and Prefrontal Chamber, Rollo is always out there, absorbing aspects of the fort only he understands. She is trapped within an extension of Rollo and somehow, within this extension, she must avoid Rollo.

...

Strewn failure surrounds Rollo. He has torn the interior of the Prefrontal Chamber apart, searching for his baby. The absurdity of his search resides within the impossible nooks in which he has directed focus. Beneath cutlery, inside cups. The layers of sheet that comprise the floor. Anything that occupies space has been examined with increasing violence. Within the frenzy, every action is rendered reasonable. A shattered plate represents only the elimination of a potential hiding place rather than the destruction of property. It never occurs to him Ingrid and his baby are not there. Rollo has underestimated Ingrid. He has projected an old pattern upon her that no longer seems to apply.

He sits among the refuse, feeling the bite of broken flotsam penetrate his skin. The frenzy leaves him in layers. Each layer injecting clarity and reassessment. With the removal of the first layer, it becomes apparent his child is not here. Time has been wasted and his attention was directed incorrectly. As the second layer of frenzy leaves, his recently concluded actions call attention to themselves. The damage he has caused. The loss of self-control. A pronounced fear weighs down his stomach and agitates the passage of blood. Consumed food begs for release, launching campaigns against him, failing, regrouping, and starting again. Rollo's stubborn body denies release. Muscles strain, closing off all exits, allowing the tumult of food to grow further agitated.

When the final layer of frenzy leaves, it is replaced with the knowledge he is now feared. Unpredictable action now defines him and, in Ingrid's eyes, he cannot be trusted. Evidence of Ingrid's newfound perspective lay around him, reinforcing and feeding. This perspective prevents access to the child. His eyes have not yet learned the language of its appearance. It exists in a whorl of abstraction reaching for impossible form.

Rollo needs to convince Ingrid he is not what she assumes him to be. Current evidence aside, he feels as a father he has much to offer. The fort stands as testament to his capability. He stands up, picking shards of broken glass and china from his skin, watching rivulets of interior ooze out. Something inside him has left. The presence of this blood is the presence of his life. When absorbed in the patterns required by the fort, there is little opportunity for Rollo to understand he possesses life. Something so fundamental. Instead he feels component in mechanizations beyond him. The thought follows that Ingrid too is in possession of a life no less complex and confusing than his. The two of them, rather than mere components, are the cause of the mechanizations they abide by. These mechanizations are themselves subject to other mechanizations. There is no end. All things feed off one another, forcing life's momentum to continue. In this dance of consumption and consumed, all things act in accordance to a balance.

The escalating incongruity represents an imbalance to the fort's welfare, which represents an imbalance to their welfare. Events are unfolding completely out of sync. Rollo must work toward the restoration of balance in whatever capacity that entails.

He scours the Prefrontal Chamber's wreckage, weeding out anything that remains intact. Surviving plates are stacked and placed carefully in cupboards. Cutlery is introduced back to its drawers. Furniture is shaken of debris and dragged to its resting position. Anything broken is pushed into a pile without consideration. Rollo does not want to understand the specifics of the damage. Specifics will only allow for the formation of attachment with the broken objects, which Rollo has no time for. This pile will be disposed of via the waste management system and forgotten. They still possess enough ephemera to ensure the continuity of their day-to-day life. Restoring order to the chamber is a step toward restoring order to their dynamic. He undertakes the restoration with care, understanding that haste cannot possibly honor the fort and what it requires. Haste is not something the fort understands.

The wounds on his body have coagulated. They will busy themselves with their own patterns and heal what was broken. Rollo no longer needs to consider them. The life of a wound is a short-lived conversation with the body. Hemostasis. Inflammation. Collagen proliferation. Contraction. New skin.

Seated in the restored order of the Frontal Chamber, Rollo allows for peace to assure him. His tired eyes are content with what they see and decide to close. They burn gently behind his eyelids, bathing in fluid until the burn soothes. With the barest commitment, he could fall asleep, but now is not the time. It is enough to enjoy the peace of relaxation before he is forced into another action.

Ingrid is out there somewhere, occupying a position in the fort. Rollo directs his focus toward the chatter of her mind, trying to find sense in her chaotic mental verbiage. If she would relinquish some of her telepathic chaos and give it to reason, Rollo would have something to work with. Instead he understands only the intonation of certain sounds. Panic. Fear. Anger. Nothing else is afforded a voice.

Regardless of the outcome, Rollo must find her. He does not imagine it will take a great deal of effort. The fort is known to him in detail. His concern is focused more on how to approach Ingrid rather than whether or not he will find her. He assumes the latter and is terrified of the former.

12.

Rollo and Ingrid once apart. The movement of one occurs without the knowledge of the other. We are pre-fort. Pre-them. They have not yet come together as a new whole. The childhood Rollo is a construction of influences and experience, all coming together as an individual. Ingrid is the same. Two separate beings aware only of their own parts.

...

When she was young enough to remember everything, before what was learned became subsumed by what is, Ingrid was given a gift by her grandmother. A towel embroidered with red stars. The towel was hers. At night it was tucked into her body, keeping them both safe in one unconscious gesture. When awake, her fingers explored the raised thread of the stars. Tracing their outline, reading their detail. Her mind consuming the embroidered stars until the stitching resided not just on the towel itself, but also within her nature.

Her grandmother would embroider, knit, cross-stitch and thread Ingrid's formation. A childhood defined by her grandmother's hands. As Ingrid's dexterity developed, her grandmother transitioned from making to teaching. Ingrid sewed her first stitch on a plain white handkerchief under her grandmother's guidance. Caring eyes savored the birth of Ingrid's aptitude. Allowing for mistakes in order to understand correction. A line of red stitches. Almost too straight for someone without experience. Taken and framed as a keepsake.

It hung on her grandmother's living room wall. It greeted Ingrid whenever she visited, always stoking aptitude's fire. Reminding her everything possesses a beginning.

The outward simplicity of the handkerchief belied its complexity. A straight line of stitches was the foundation upon which the development of Ingrid's ability sat. From here, her capability blossomed, allowing greater execution. Her stitching was now dictated by what she could imagine rather than the limitations of ability. Patterns were stitched. Shapes were knitted. Her family soon wore sweaters and scarves forged by Ingrid's hands.

Ingrid was in a possession of an ability she was already beginning to forget the origins of. We often forget how we learned what we know. The act of doing has little time to remember why it can do. Textile skill worked to define who Ingrid was. Learning the skill served no purpose outside of attaining the skill. Learning can and should be continual, but progress rarely reaches toward its beginning.

Her father was a plumber. From an indistinct time before Ingrid was born to the moment she left for the fort, plumbing remained his profession. This instilled a fascination of pipe systems within Ingrid. The mystery of a world existing below them, ceaseless in activity, designed to work beyond the scope of casual sight. Her father's life was dedicated to pipes that disobeyed their design. So much of his world unfolded within this invisible world. His job was forcing pipes to re-obey their design. To carry water deeper into a system Ingrid longed to understand.

Ingrid was washing her face in the bathroom. She removed the plug and watched the unmoving soapy water, which refused to disappear into the plughole. This contradicted one of her basic understandings. The hole at the bottom of the sink existed to remove used water. She kept vigil over the strange spectacle, beginning to notice the water level was, almost beyond perception, decreasing. It seemed the sink was sick and

Ingrid wanted to know how to make it better. The hole that took the water no longer appeared endless. She became aware of something bigger controlling the hole. A system. The water emerging from the tap obeyed a process that allowed its passage into the sink. When the plug was removed, it depended on another process to carry it away. When one process within the machine ceased, the whole machine ceased. The fragility of these integrated processes overwhelmed Ingrid.

She watched her father dismantle the pipe that refused her unwanted water. He fed strange instruments into the plughole and performed mysterious hand movements. The instruments would emerge covered in black slime and hair. Before this moment, Ingrid erased everything that traveled down the hole from her mind, as if the act removed it from existence. This was no longer the case. Everything the hole took went on to continue its own type of existence in this pipe world.

The specific abilities of her father were akin to magic. Before this moment, she was unaware of her father as anything but her father. Now he was someone who had a function beyond her. He was someone capable of amazing things. When he had completed his magic, water once again travelled down the hole unimpeded. He put his strange instruments away, changed out of his overalls and was, once again, Ingrid's father. Almost as though he had not been responsible for the orchestration of impossible things.

Ingrid studied water running from taps simply to marvel at its passage. A part of her longed for the sink to become ill once more so she could watch her father perform this role outside her father. She remembered the black hairy slime that had been removed when it was sick and fed hair and mud into its depths, hoping to trigger an upset in the pipe world. When she succeeded, her excitement was outweighed by the anger of her father who, in this strange moment, was both the father she knew and the man capable of the magic she longed to witness. This duality taught Ingrid that people could exist, even in the same moment, as more than one thing.

    Following this awakening, Ingrid developed an acute awareness of pipe systems, understanding them by pure will. It became impossible for her to encounter one without seeing the world beyond it. Pipes that led to pipes that led to pipes. She started observing her father more carefully, hoping to learn his magic, following him around, asking questions. Questions he had no great interest in answering at first. As his daughter's odd interest became unavoidable, he started feeding her the craved information. Sometimes the information would underwhelm, but as she reflected upon what she had been told, the possibilities unfolded before her. On weekends her father would take Ingrid along to jobs, as an observer at first, then as a participant for the less complex duties. As aptitude developed, the responsibility bestowed upon her increased.

...

These were just two of the many facets that formed the pre-Rollo Ingrid. Facets that contributed to the girl Rollo fell in love with. Rollo, of course, possessed many facets of his own, contributing to the boy Ingrid fell in love with. When the two came together, so did their individual facets, merging into the development of a new whole. In the love they shared, their identities meshed together without seams. They were so immersed in the eddies of the other's ocean, that nothing about their own ocean sought protection. Each was granted total access and explored the other's depths, forming new opinions. Long-held selves were deconstructed and rebuilt in the other's image. Rollo translated and deconstructed the deepest locales of Ingrid through the deepest locales of him, unaware his deepest locales were undergoing the same process via Ingrid's translation. Each pulled the other toward them, shaving off differences, coming together. Stepping away from themselves in a drive toward the emergence of new self derived of the two.

Of the shaved parts… those demarcating a facet incompatible with the whole's operation, they are obscured but forever extant. They are ghosts of a person past, pushed aside rather than deleted. Ghosts that hold eternities in which to haunt. Already dead, so incapable of dying.

Jellyfish Reproduction

A male jellyfish will spawn each day. Releasing clouds of sperm into the surrounding ocean. Seeking out a host prepared to grant it fertilization. Colliding and becoming something new. Planulae develop and are released by the female, where it floats through the water like dust in forgotten houses. Their float is trapped within the ocean's dictation, edging downward, finally meeting with objects on the ocean floor. As polyps they fuse with these objects. In this position they can lie dormant for decades. Life exists somewhere within them. Waiting. Unhurried.

Patience consumes the polyp. It obeys a pattern unconcerned with anything else. When deemed appropriate, the polyp will undertake strobilation, reproducing in and of itself. Casting off others just like it, introducing myriad selves to its world. Selves which understand and continue the pattern. These polyps build a rudimentary form of their final selves. The rudimentary selves embrace the constant cloud of plankton. They gorge on the plankton, growing, becoming more. Jellyfish, as we understand them, are formed.

These jellyfish will continue the drift dictated by the ocean, gorging on plankton without end, increasing in size. Obsessed with the continuation of their pattern. Unable to obey anything else.

...

Ghosts float through live wires. Seeking connection with something able to explain why the ghost was born. Rollo and

Ingrid took openly from one another. Replacing what had been taken with what they were taking until the only place they could find themselves was in each other.

Eventually one will seek a part of their self not accounted for by the other. This part reaches into their past. Before they became one half of a whole. When all they were was individual.

Discarded pasts lie dormant. They never cease their wait. Understanding, better than the one who created them, that they may be needed. They remain in place for their host who must seek them out. At the end of circuitous routes. The culmination of aimless searching. A deep part of the self never truly forgotten, merely removed from comprehension. When the host discovers this past, its dormancy ceases. A process begins where, once more, the two become one. A fragment of self now exists external to the relationship that has defined them. This wayward fragment once more finds refuge within the host. The two conspire against the relationship in blissful whispers. The past is reintroduced in the guise of a new present. Steady trajectories are altered. Even when lost to what feels like stasis, nothing remains the same.

13.

Ingrid suspects the Central Sulcus Emergency Tunnel is conspiring against her. It wears the disguise of disuse. The dust coating the Sulcus Tunnel smells false. It smells disturbed. Acting to mask what she believes is Rollo's frequent occupation of the space.

One cannot invent the sadness of neglect. It grows slowly over time, allowing for the possibility of care's intervention. Hopeful. Naïve. Assured that it will be discovered and removed. Neglect is both a process and an endpoint. One that slowly chokes hope until it dies. Ingrid studies the dust on her fingertips, unable to locate the neglect it should suggest. The tunnel is a lie. It was conceived as a trap by Rollo, who somehow foresaw this moment. A moment that would require Ingrid's immobilization.

The baby is pressed harder against Ingrid's chest as she works to calm it with the internal song of her biology. To soothe it with the beat of her heart, trying to mask her panic so the baby cannot feel it. There are few chambers in the fort inaccessible from the Sulcus Tunnel, therefore there are few chambers in the fort that do not lead to Ingrid.

Rollo will find them both. How can there be any other outcome? For Ingrid to avoid him successfully, she would have to move in endless circles from one chamber to the next. A perpetual movement, unsustainable over any timeframe. This movement would necessitate Rollo adhering to a pattern understood by Ingrid, which seems impossible in the face of his newfound unpredictability. Each attempt to formulate a plan is hindered by the imagined visage of Rollo obstructing mental progress. Ingrid's precious son has understood nothing but the fear preoccupying its mother. Only one outcome must be considered… the safety of the baby. An action cannot exist that Ingrid will not consider in order to achieve this outcome. Whether considering the action will result in performing the action is another matter beyond Ingrid's ability to comprehend.

Ingrid's head tilts backward, just enough to survey the ceiling of the Sulcus Tunnel. Beyond the ceiling, through layers of compressed soil, exists something that is not the fort. Whatever life before the fort consisted of continues to interact with an aboveground world detached from everything she knows. If it meant the safety of her child, would Ingrid join her unknown past aboveground? The thought congeals within Ingrid. Slowing. Fighting movement. Melting into pure fear. Her memory is unable to locate further instances of this thought. In the emergence of this moment, Ingrid cannot understand how leaving the fort has never been afforded focus. While her intellect is capable of acknowledging life removed from the fort, instinct has forbidden this acknowledgment from merging with intention. Even now, as paranoia and fear for her child's safety scream like frightened animals, she is unable to invoke the required intention. Whatever course of action Ingrid chooses must limit itself to the confines of her world. What exists aboveground ceased being her world long before the memory of this time disappeared. Her eyes abort their study of the ceiling.

Limits have been set. The course of action will occur in the fort. Evasion is a plan that lacks longevity. Rather than evade Rollo, Ingrid must confront him. Stop him. Rollo's mobility cannot continue.

It would be possible, if Ingrid exercised commitment, to end Rollo's life. It is a thought that sits more comfortably than she is comfortable with, but she allows the thought to explore itself. Life, in all its iterations, will move toward its end. The end it moves toward could, without a great deal of complication, be introduced in a deliberate fashion. Ingrid could use the life within her to take the life within Rollo. The pure mechanics of the task are not beyond anyone. Prolonged periods of safety lose connection with life's fragility. The continuation of life transcends expectation and exists beyond comprehension. If we have enjoyed a prolonged period of safety, how can we conceptualize the end of that period? It is only in moments defined by illness or danger that life reveals its tenuous hold on continuation.

As Ingrid envisions the act of killing Rollo, the thought transforms into something horrific. The sensation of a knitting needle as it penetrates Rollo's skin, even in mere thought, triggers pain within Ingrid, as if she were committing the imagined act against the self. Her body experiences pain as the needle's penetration shifts. Ingrid endeavors to move away from these thoughts, but slips backward, becoming smothered by them. Her imagined acts of violence, in every sense but their physicality, become real until her whole body writhes in pain. The theoretical act is subsumed by its emotional weight until one more potential course of action is erased from her list. Only when every part of Ingrid believes she will not kill Rollo does the stabbing pain cease.

Without solution, Ingrid feels helpless. She is unable to remove herself and the baby from the fort. She is unable to remove Rollo from the fort. The outcome she seeks is bound to the environment she seeks it in. The three of them will remain here because there is nowhere else. Rollo will remain alive because murder cannot exist within her. All that remains is to incapacitate Rollo. This in itself is not the conclusion to Ingrid's worry; rather it is a means of buying time.

The Central Sulcus Emergency Tunnel is equipped with a security system that can be activated to incapacitate any intruders. Once activated, the Sulcus Tunnel initiates lockdown and disperses infectious spores throughout all other chambers in the fort. On a theoretical level, the system is an ingenious safety net, allowing for their continuation. In the realm of practicality, the system has never been employed. The method by which one activates the security system lacks clarity in Ingrid's mind. It was, like most things in the fort, designed and implemented by Rollo. It strikes Ingrid as a strange act of cruelty to seek Rollo's incapacitation via his own invention, but somehow, also fitting.

She navigates toward the top of the tunnel, holding her baby closer than ever, with absence of mind, trying to force it into her belly. Into the space that exists within a woman where a baby is supposed to grow. A life projected upon an inanimate object, which cannot help but oblige the unconscious desires of the living object imbuing it with more than it can ever be.

Seven velvet ropes hang from the tunnel's ceiling. Three red. Two yellow. Two white. Each rope hangs at a different length from the others. They control mechanisms deep within the hidden layers of the fort. There is an order to these ropes that, when abided by, should result in the system's deployment. The order required by the ropes is something she knows, but it exists in decrepit fragments of memory. The fragments have scattered like dandelion florets in the wind. Each floret possesses data different from the others. Individually useless. Of value only in dialogue with its sibling florets.

Sifting through memory, searching for fragments relating to the totality of Ingrid's life. Fragments are placed side-by-side. Continuity between fragments is sought. One hand remains pressed against the baby; the other combs Ingrid's beard with spanned fingers. Each rigid follicle presses against the palm of her hand, investigating the skin. Hand leaves beard and reaches toward the first rope. Red. Second longest. Potentially incorrect. The hand closes around the rope and pulls down. The rope plays at resisting, but gives without a great deal of exertion. Dust from the tunnel's ceiling is dislodged and floats downward in slow pendulous arcs, seeking Ingrid's nostrils. A series of clockwork sounds click and rattle within the walls. A sound that may be a ball bearing travels on a track around the tunnel's circumference. It drops into something wet. A series of long, thick woolen blankets fall around Ingrid, covering the tunnel's surface.

Ingrid reaches toward another rope. White. The shortest. It has less give than the first and threatens Ingrid's footing as she pulls. When the rope obeys, Ingrid hears something that could be a sheet of steel falling above her. The fall shakes the tunnel, dislodging more dust. Rather than fight it, she allows it to enter her as it deems appropriate, choosing instead to consider the remaining ropes. The dust infiltrates Ingrid, marking its entry with unreachable irritation.

Although the memory has been forbidden access, something communicating at an unknown level is aware of the pattern. Before Ingrid moved to the fort, before she and Rollo became one, her life was consistent with that of most people her age. After school, she would spend her evenings on the phone with those she was just at school with. Gossip too precarious to utter in the presence of the group was saved for one-on-one telephone encounters. Each friend was privy to a different fragment of gossip. Each fragment, when stitched together, told the schoolyard's overarching narrative.

The phone number of each friend never existed inside Ingrid's consciousness. The numbers lived in her fingertips, where they followed a pattern equal to the correct sequence of numbers. It was only by refusing to engage her conscious that she was able to dial the correct sequence of numbers correctly. When attention was cast upon the number, it would form a jumble from which the pattern could not be discerned.

The pattern of the ropes exists as the phone numbers of her childhood. Only by forgetting she needs to know the pattern will she be able to execute the pattern. Ingrid senses this, but cannot give form to it. She steps away from herself, allowing an automated process to engage. Beyond her outstretched arm, there is nothing except absent movement. She feels rope in her hand but refuses to understand the rope. As one rope gives, her hand moves to another. Each new rope triggers sounds around the tunnel that betray its inner life. When the final rope is pulled, sliding metal can be heard around her. This is followed by a hiss with the aural properties of escaping steam.

Throughout the tunnel, spores fill the air.

...

Rollo stimulates his salivary glands, attempting to fill his drying mouth with something to spit over the mirrors in the Occipital Chamber. Were the mirrors merely dirty, they could be fixed. Something easily rectified to restore reflective clarity. They display little more than abstract textures. Any one of the mirrors may, somewhere within their indefinite array of merging shapes, reflect Ingrid and his hypothetical baby. He studies them with increasing focus, as if focus in and of itself can create detail.

Rollo shares a dialogue with the fort. The ways in which Ingrid betrays her location are all communicated by the fort. It would be so easy to find her. Almost a game, like hide-and-seek with a child, but Rollo has had predatory intent projected upon him. Ingrid's every action has sought to reinforce this projection, and he has allowed himself to become it. He needs to withdraw from Ingrid's manipulation. Shift the dynamic.

Rollo's face meets the cool glass of a surveillance mirror. Its uselessness mocks him, introducing Rollo to his own vast ignorance. This carefully constructed, self-congratulatory system possesses no concrete purpose beyond his aggrandizement. Whoever Rollo was before he became all he remembers, at some level, must have assumed this surveillance system would never meet its function. A useless accoutrement, worn by the fort as a fashion statement. What other functional dimensions of the fort in actuality lack function? Existing only to bolster the ego of whoever that version of Rollo was. To what fraudulence has he dedicated his life to maintaining without question? His dialogue with the fort has never ventured into this territory. The fort only understands the construction bestowed upon it.

He is sickened and enraged, longing to reach into his past

and inflict pain upon this forgotten earlier self. Wanting to drag this self into the present, forcing him to see how useless his invention is. To parade him before it, stripping him of his ill-gained confidence. Replacing the self-importance with the doubt of intelligence.

He raises his face from the mirror and brings it down again with force, feeling shudders of impact travel through the blood. The movement is repeated. Harder. The impact more severe. Repeated. Harder. Harder. Harder. He continues to perform this simple movement until the impact cracks the mirror. He lifts his face to examine what has been achieved. Layers of smudged blood obscure reflection further. Rollo's face burns with pain his hands lack the courage to touch. The warm wet of newly struck blood travels the curve of his neck. Into the collar of his clothing.

Slumped against the wall, Rollo removes his shirt, peeling its dampness away and discarding it on the ground. Attention is paid to the jut of his breasts. The sensitivity of his nipples, which seem engorged, almost painful to touch. He cups each breast, feeling their weight, wondering what they are for. If they serve an unexplored purpose. Pressure is applied to each and builds within. The action is accompanied by discomfort, but it does not feel wrong. Two jets of colostrum emerge from the tips of Rollo's nipples, painting the ground around him.

…

We refuse to acknowledge the bulk of who we are. Conflict abounds between emergence and suppression in all things. Raw feeling and thought are born and sculpted into a fathomed unit before our conscious understanding is permitted to interact with it. The process separating who we are from who we *really* are enables us to form relationships with ourselves and, eventually, with each other. Relationships based upon the interaction of lies. This dynamic is known. Anyone who understands the extent of what they suppress from others understands the extent of what is suppressed from them. A relationship, in order to operate with continuity, must nurture the continuity of suppression. The relationship with others, and with the self.

The equilibrium of continuity can fall victim to life's traumas, permitting remnants of raw feeling to infiltrate the manicured environment of our conscious garden. Wild flowers break through the soil, severing root systems, dominating what we have carefully planted. Burdening the landscape, tempting it toward discord. The chaotic whorl of unconscious truth flows through the tempered conscious. Once known, it is integral. Something we must assimilate into the evolution of who we are.

...

Rollo has become aware an integral component of everything he knows is amiss. It communicates with him using language similar to Ingrid's psychic wordlessness. It expresses via feeling and casts shadows he cannot escape. Something is reaching into the past and withdrawing alien fragments that want to make sense.

The fort keeps truths Rollo did not know to look for. Truths beyond the process of its upkeep. The walls vibrate with his past. With Ingrid's past. With their past. Everything that was forgotten lives inside the fort, following them, longing to rejoin them. Memory and truth seek each other out, imploring Rollo to facilitate this reunion.

The point at which experience gives way to memory is gradated, bleeding together the many thens and nows. Memory begins constructing its own truth before the experience responsible for the memory's creation ends. Defining lines are an illusion. Something has happened to Rollo and Ingrid that contradicts their past, so incongruous that memory has completely abandoned them. They have responded with escape, unable to confront whatever called them forth.

Rollo steps out of the Occipital Chamber, determined to

communicate the enormity of his doubt with Ingrid. Seeking out a place beyond conflict where the potential for communication might exist. In the time since the concept of the baby, Rollo has learned to hate Ingrid. Despising her for stepping away from the routine and introducing new beginnings. Before this hate, he considers what existed between the two of them, understanding it to be simple absence. Rollo cannot escape the sense that at one point the two of them were close. Potentially one. Coiled around the foundations of each other. Driven forward by the same heart. Something occurred that triggered a separation, dividing their shared whole like cells lost in mitosis. Poorly rendered facsimiles of a dynamic that suffocated itself out of existence. If he can place his words in the right order when speaking to Ingrid, he may be able to bypass the countless layers of hatred they feel. This is not about a baby. The baby is counterfeit. Ingrid's attachment to the baby is counterfeit. Rollo's attachment to the fort is counterfeit. The only attachment not lacking an essential core of truth *may* have been the one Rollo and Ingrid had for each other.

Each step Rollo takes toward Ingrid, wherever she may be, feels labored, as though the air is composed differently. His airways are beginning to swell and it feels like fur is breaking through the surface of his lungs. His tongue burns with a foreign taste. His stomach convulses, searching for food to cast out and finds nothing. Particles of pink glow dance above him like dead insects floating without purpose to the ground below. Filling the fort's dim with a new hue, beautiful in its quietly ominous way.

Rollo manages the barest smile as an artificial version of pre-sleep weakens each limb. His eyelids join in slow motion blinks, unable to continue. Ingrid has activated the security system in the Central Sulcus Tunnel and Rollo has fallen its victim. His smile finds fuller form as an unnatural sleep steals him.

14.

Ingrid fails to understand the benefits of doing so, but she ties up Rollo's unconscious bulk. The knots consist of hurried entanglements that appear complex, but threaten to unravel without difficulty. Until now, Ingrid's concern has been occupied with incapacitating Rollo. A singular outcome easily assimilated. With that task completed, the more problematic component of her dilemma shifts into focus. What now? Enclosed as they are in the fort, where does one seek genuine refuge? The fort itself was conceived as refuge, but now represents anything but. A deeper refuge is required. One that protects the baby by separating Ingrid from Rollo.

Without the presence of life, Rollo appears benign. Pathetic. Utterly inessential. Ingrid wonders where his newfound ability to terrify her resides in this mass of warm flesh. What does a person possess that makes them anything? Perhaps as an excuse to avoid the futility of her plan, she considers Rollo might not be so dangerous after all. Whatever it was that brought the two together cannot have appeared dangerous. A time must have existed wherein the two felt safe together. Safe enough to occupy the fort without the need of another. Ingrid once found comfort in this man.

She picks up her baby, carefully holding it before her, staring into its eyes, determined to do right. Its head tilts to one side, as if lost in confusion. Ingrid tilts her head to match.

"What would you do if you were me?" she says to her baby.

It maintains its frozen confusion, as if Ingrid had said nothing.

"Is this someone you want to know?"

She turns around so Rollo's tied form sits in the baby's line of sight. It shows no sign of comprehension.

"If it were up to me, I would keep him away from you. I love you too much to see you get hurt. I am not saying this man would hurt you, but I am not sure he would not."

Ingrid longs to see something inside the baby that responds to her love. Her life has forgotten what it means to feel loved. Ingrid has so much love within her. It pushes at her seams, begging for release. A bucket in which to fill. It sometimes feels as though her body may buckle beneath the enormity of her unexpressed love. It is love she cannot simply give away. It must be felt and returned. Unreturned love is quick to find hate. Hate is easily returned. Often in greater abundance than it was given.

She shakes the baby ever so gently.

"I wish you would do something," she says. "I love you so much. I want to be so good to you."

More strength is directed toward shaking her baby. Its head tilts from side-to-side, but still betrays nothing.

"Do something," she repeats, giving her voice more volume. "If you want your father to be a part of you, just tell me. Smile. Blink. Anything. I do not want to prevent you from what you want."

The baby remains steadfast in its lifelessness. Tears bead at the edge of Ingrid's eyes, gaining weight and falling. If the baby could find love for Rollo, it would allow Ingrid to indulge her own.

"I just want you to love me," she whispers, afraid that Rollo will somehow hear.

Still. Nothing. Ingrid is left with her own frayed perception. With legs crossed, she places the baby on her lap and watches Rollo. His stillness is a lie. When Ingrid trains her vision on specific locales of his bodily environment, there is nothing still. Even while unconscious, Rollo is an ecosystem hosting a complex array of life.

Eyelids:
Engage in spasmodic flutters as though fending off light from invisible suns. Light that perhaps Rollo recalls from a past that may not have been.

Nostrils:
Flare as though locked in combat with oxygen, forcing it inside, altering its structure and expelling it as something else. Something damaged and wrong.

Chest:
Rises and falls in slow patterns sending ghosts of movement down each limb. Fed by the nostrils. Connected to breathing mechanisms. Destroying the oxygen. Casting it off. Commanding more.

Skin:
Finds goose bumps within and invites them to the surface. Arrectores pilorum squeezing and engorging each hair. Rollo's unconscious performs a childhood song that never asked to be forgotten. Not invented by his mother, but made important via her translation and sung to Rollo prior to bed on the nights she understood happiness.

Nipples:
Leak the newly discovered colostrum. Blue-hued nutrient wasted to the ground. Runnels joining a pool beneath Rollo's body. Absorbed in part by the skin.

Mouth:
Used by the sleep sounds to articulate something dancing inside. Useless noise detached from communication.

Ingrid:
Squeezing into the anti-baby on her lap with jealous fingers.

Wishing to capture the constant signs of Rollo's life and feed it to her attempted offspring.

Rollo plays his life like a detuned instrument Ingrid does not want to hear. Even in sleep it seems he mocks her child. Parading what it means to feel life in the presence of one who cannot. The fort creaks and wheezes from somewhere above, becoming another thing that seems more alive than her child. Always engaged in a hidden process. A programmed action. Something at some point designed by them.

"We will get through this," she whispers to her baby. "Do not pay any attention to him. You do not need to be what he is. You are alive in your own special way. A way you will reveal to me when you are ready. I will look after you. I will look after you."

Ingrid stares at the walls, understanding that within them exists unexplored space. A hidden world within their hidden world. A world divorced from Rollo. Divorced from them. A place Ingrid can start anew with her baby. This unexplored space offers an opportunity to feel safety.

It is unknown how long Rollo will remain unconscious, so Ingrid feels compelled to act. Within the self-imposed limitations, she has a course of action that promises a way forward. She pushes the baby once more into the smooth of her stomach and edges toward Rollo. The tip of her tongue coats her lips with wetness before slipping back into the safety of the mouth. Ingrid shivers under the weight of this unfolding moment. Her lips find Rollo's forehead. Their proximities, for one moment, merge into a single occupation of luxuriant space. Rollo's skin feels warm, and transfers a film of sweat to Ingrid's lips, which her tongue cannot help but taste. It is the sweat of fever dreams and reconstituting mental architecture. Sweat manufactured within the deepest heart of his heart. Sweat Ingrid feels like a thief for tasting.

She moves her lips to Rollo's ear canal and directs a whisper that tickles his cilia.

"I do not think I can kill the part of me that loves you, but I promise I will never stop trying. Please do not look for us. Let the baby and I be what we need to be."

Ingrid's mouth closes before she has a chance to whisper 'goodbye.' It is not a word she feels she can live up to. 'Goodbye' is the most dishonest word language has conjured. It is a muscle we flex to intimidate and impress. A word without flesh. Goodbye is simply a word preceding hello. To truly leave another, one must never seek contact again. Only death is goodbye.

Ingrid leaves Rollo alone in the Parietal Chamber, refusing to look back, as though such an action will trigger a series of events antithetical to everything she needs to feel. She scales the Medulla Shaft until she stands at its base, the vibration of waste management below. The baby is tucked into the waist of her skirt, enabling both hands to perform the next task.

She searches for edges on the blankets comprising the walls. When an edge is found, it is carefully peeled back, until the next layer reveals itself. The process continues, Ingrid's hands uncovering layer after layer, each movement careful in the hope it can be reversed, masking Ingrid's entry into the walls.

Persistence finds the point where blankets end and hollow space begins. Grey light exists within this hollow space and Ingrid crawls toward it, trying not to wonder where the light is coming from. It is because things are, and that is enough for Ingrid.

The blankets are easier to peel away than set back in place. Forcing them back into position requires Ingrid's hands to exhibit great care and patience. Layer by layer her entry point disappears until there is no entry point. Signs of the wall's disruption, however minute, will be visible to Rollo. Ingrid does not imagine any effort to hide from Rollo could truly prevent him from finding her should it be what he desires, but why would anyone desire something that avoids them with such commitment?

...

Two gears become transmission when working together. Each gear wearing cogs around the circumference that mesh together when engaged in their purpose. Each cog forms a relationship during each rotation. The repetition of these brief relationships is the totality of that function. The cogs enable the gears to continue their rotation, feeding their transmission into another mechanism. While the machine is alive, the sequence of mechanisms within the machine understand only their own totality, unaware they are enabling another function separate to them. This fandango of function is unaware of the dance it performs. These functions are organs in the machine's body, keeping it alive. A gear that does not rotate is a gear occupying useless space. A gear wants nothing but to rotate.

...

Ingrid beholds the towering skeletons of dead machinery climbing the space within the fort's walls. Browning steel interlocked in stasis. Fossils of function. Archaeological remnants of former lives. The scope of the mechanical construction fixes Ingrid in place, commanding her attention away from the baby and into the world of its overwhelming detail. Everything is connected to what precedes it, advancing beyond Ingrid's line of sight, suggesting an endless parade of forgotten process.

Ingrid moves through the space, taking in new components of the machine. Its stillness disquiets her. In this stillness there is anger. The desire to scream with life. To feel the dirt and pain of work. The drive to exist as anything but unused and forgotten. Whether this is a feeling fed by the machine or projected by Ingrid, it is one she feels an affinity with.

Ingrid is aware everything before her is something, in part, built by her. Together with Rollo, each component in this machine was set in place with a purpose. A forgotten plan. Her brain fires memory requests, each one returned unfilled. Beyond all else, Ingrid is drawn toward waking the machinery. Whatever mechanism is set in place to power this steel sculpture is as lost to her memory as its existence.

She approaches a gear that matches her height and places her foot on one of its cogs. Above the gear is another, which is attached to another and another. She starts to ascend the steel, feeling the harshness of its surface against her skin. The machine is scaled without understood purpose. Finding the next foothold is process enough to fuel her momentum.

The machine draws her in, introducing a world within the world she thought she knew. There is majesty in its construction contradicting the callow assemblage of the pillow world. As though the world of blankets and pillows are a façade concealing the importance of whatever this inner world means.

In the continued exploration of this steel environment, Ingrid's attention leaves the baby. It sits unconsidered against her stomach, absorbed into her anatomy. Like an organ one only comprehends when it falters and upsets the body's operation. The area within her thought process dedicated to the baby has fallen asleep. The area concerned with Rollo's pursuit has done the same. There is only the operation of the machine.

Devices with the appearance of levers are pulled, but refuse to understand what Ingrid hopes of them. A crank is turned, but meets resistance before it can complete a single rotation. It seems somewhere within the belly of this rusted structure must exist something willing to experience life. All things reach toward their purpose and a machine should be no different.

She scales higher, disorienting her sense of space. Losing any connection to where she resides in relation to everything else. Unaware her baby has slipped slightly in her waistband. Unaware that she sought refuge in the walls for a reason. She climbs toward a clearing in the mechanical jumble where the uniformity of dim light finds the independence of greater illumination. The clearing possesses a steel grate base in which Ingrid can stand.

The exertion of ascent had gone unnoticed until now, so much so that Ingrid resents stopping. Admiring that part of her is capable of directing attention away from discomfort. Away from anything not pertaining to an immediate goal.

Had she not spotted the mushroom-shaped red button protruding from the wall, her thought process would have moved from the leg pain to the well-being of her baby. Instead, her attention is refocused on the goal. The button sits alone in the steel environment, conspicuous and calling for intervention. She studies her palm before pressing it against the button.

The introduction of force does little to tempt the button into relinquishing its stasis, so Ingrid applies more. The barest hint of movement. Enough to continue. She places her second hand atop her first and applies greater force with both. Another flirtation with movement. She anchors her front foot in the interest of increased force.

The button gives in, slamming downward, casting off dust.

At first, nothing. Ingrid turns in a slow circle, hoping to see new life. From above, what sounds like a sheet of steel tumbles down an unseen shaft, rattling like a dying vehicle. It collides with the ground. The sound of reverberating impact destabilizes Ingrid's footing. She lurches backward, searching for balance. Unaware the baby has slipped from her waistband and now sits by her feet.

Yawning sounds beneath her as the machinery wakes into its first new day in memory. The dislodgement of sediment. The reversal of stasis. An industrial cacophony booms, encouraging Ingrid's fingers to protect her ears. The components around her all find their individual voice. Gears rotate. Pistons pump. Drums spin. It is only now, having achieved her goal, that Ingrid affords attention to her baby. She pats her stomach and feels internal free fall when the vacant waistband is revealed. She fights against the growing cloud of panic in the interest of a measured approach to the dilemma, but finds the cloud dominating and smothering. Her screams are absorbed into the surrounding soundscape. Useless. Her eyes dart with erratic jerks, too frenzied to capture detail. She feels something beneath the shuffle of her feet and jerks her vision downward. The baby lies unconcerned. She maneuvers into position to collect it, but does so with haste, and kicks it aside. The baby falls. Ingrid dives too late to prevent, but just in time to watch as it becomes savaged by two meshing gears. Its stuffing erupts. The material consumed. It is destroyed without effort. All Ingrid can manage is an empty stare, which she directs through her environment and into something else.

15.

Rollo's brain is not quite ready to relinquish its unconsciousness. The spores have nestled deep, installing mental cotton, insulating this from that. Painting detail with torpid blur. The booming rhythmic clatter of awakened machinery troubles the air, filling the fort with new sound. The interjection of any new element to a known environment forces a reassessment of that environment. Until this moment, the aural qualities of the fort wore the illusion of silence. There was no shortage of sound in their world, but it was an unchanging symphony that, over time, had drifted away from attention.

The sound of machinery screaming within the walls is too new. A new symphony drowning out the old. Following the requirements of an unknown conductor. Too loud to understand. Too loud to ignore. The louder a sound is, the more difficult it can be to hear. Sleep has knocked that from this, failing to prevent the entrance of sound. Rollo is forced toward the waking world. Pulled from the spores' fog. An unnatural extraction severing sleep's roots in violent jerks.

Rollo's eyes blink open, but see nothing except for spikes of grating sound. Lightning bolts of waveform dancing about the retina in deafening strobes. His mouth opens and sucks at oxygen. Greedy gasps. Aerating his body. He does not comprehend where he is. For one moment, there is no fort. There has never been a fort. There is no him. No Ingrid. Waking up naked into a new expanse that calls toward translation.

A glimmer of something familiar. The hem of a blue blanket in the Parietal Chamber. One his hands have mended before.

Possibly more than once. Rollo reaches a hand toward it, attempting to draw further cognizance into his body. The taste of sleep coats his dried white tongue and a ball of pressure presses against the front of his skull. The poison of intoxicated slumber has accompanied Rollo into the waking world of new sound and familiar objects. The cut on his head has coagulated into slugs of blood. Brown, oxidized wound leakage coats hemispheres of his body, reminding him of recent events, pulling him further into now.

He sits up and fights the urge to fall back down. The insistent sound from within the walls is the only thing he is unable to place. The boggling extent of its reach. The way it occupies every direction so fully. The determination with which it goes about whatever it is doing. He spends time searching out a pattern as a means of assimilating it into reality. In the hope he can push it aside and focus on Ingrid.

He reaches the quick conclusion the activity within the walls is something Ingrid is responsible for. Perhaps as a means of escape, she has entered this discarded space and discovered whatever is responsible for the sound. Through the din, Rollo is unable to discern Ingrid's psychic chatter, the absence of which unnerves him. It is the only time in memory he has lost connection with her. It has become more important than ever to find her. To engage in a dialogue. Something between the two of them that bears the elusive mark of truth. Truth, whatever that word means, must find a way to prevail. Together they must experiment with something new or, perhaps more accurately, something very old.

...

The fort means nothing if its foundation is divorced from truth. Whatever led these two people into the depths of the earth must have possessed a significant meaning. There must have been a time where the two of them were bound by genuine regard for the other. Rollo is determined to reconnect with this past and embody it in the present. He has to believe that within Ingrid is the same determination. Believing anything else suggests the end of everything his life has been in accordance with. The concept of one must be reintroduced to the other.

Rollo is prepared to undo his life's work if it means finding something which represents unity between he and Ingrid. He will, if the situation requires it, tear away every blanket, stripping the fort bare of its illusion, exposing whatever resides at its core. In whatever nook Ingrid hides, he will find and reach out to her. Their dynamic will be dismantled into raw product, and then rebuilt according to a forgotten blueprint. Distance eradicated. Mutuality in all things *them*. Rollo will tear the fort apart if it means bringing him and Ingrid together.

He listens beyond the mechanical thump and scrape, directing his focus toward that which has always been there. That which he has ignored. The subsumed presence of Ingrid searching for prominence. Something demarcating Ingrid swells Rollo's senses. He arcs attention in the direction, but finds, like the mechanical awakening, it has no sole locus; rather it coats each direction. It is a glimmer. Potentially false. Invented by Rollo's hope. It is sadness and horror. Incalculable loss. He allows his mind to fill with compassion and care, hoping it is something Ingrid will feel. Something she will respond to. Now is the time for their mental conversation to find a mutual language.

Starting in the Parietal Chamber, Rollo disrupts the careful placement of blankets, cleaving through each layer and letting them fall without consideration. The time dedicated to maintaining them, the lifetime of care and workmanship, is reversed. In this care and workmanship lives everything abandoned. The sense of self. The passage of time. The significance of history. His connection to Ingrid. These are things he wishes to hold once more, and he will seek them out by undoing that which orchestrated their disappearance.

Rollo's frantic hands reach the hollow space between the

chambers, spilling antiquated air. The hive of mechanical apparatus perform their dance, inviting Rollo to understand their purpose. To join them in their ambiguous celebration. He wants to immerse himself in whatever they mean, but cannot give himself to the urge. There can only be Ingrid.

More blankets are peeled away like stubborn husks protecting fruit, altering the environment until the Parietal Chamber has lost an entire wall. Blankets give way to webs of scaffolding. The true nature of everything that has surrounded Rollo for so long is being revealed. Something that might be surprise introduces itself. Surprise is a capacity Rollo no longer understands. A capacity Rollo replaced with infinite predictability, as though emotional spikes were a detriment to the fort process. These dormant spikes are pushing to the surface, longing to re-join Rollo's emotional discourse. Surprise will be understood. There will not be an emotional limb that does not feel the rush of fresh blood.

Every scrap of useless material is removed from the Parietal Chamber, until the chamber itself knows no separation from the hollowed walls that surround it. His new walls are machinery. Forgotten memories marching toward recall. Ingrid is a part of this machinery. A part of every process that radiates function. He thinks about her name. He knows her name. Her name is one that has been held hostage on the rigid tip of Rollo's tongue. A name exists to be uttered. To be heard. All names must be heard. Ingrid's name exists in the same breath as Rollo's.

"Ingrid," he whispers into the body of the expansive machinery.

"Ingrid," he repeats with greater volume.

"Ingrid."

"Ingrid."

"Ingrid."

"Ingrid."

"Ingrid."

"Ingrid."

"Ingrid. You need to come out now. You need to be here with me. With have so much to talk about. We have lost so much time."

Rollo's voice finds no reply.

Rollo closes his eyes, seeing the fort in detail his capacity for vision cannot possess. The sound of the machinery makes sense now. He can feel the rhythm, adjusting the beat of his heart to match. Feeling a new synchronicity with a truer fort. Everything has a pattern. One needs only pay attention and it will make itself known. Now he can work with the sound in a place that does not understand the distraction. He is prepared to strip each chamber bare, but feels this will take more time than he wishes to spend. Ingrid will make herself known. Rollo's only job is to allow Ingrid to do so. His eyes shut tighter, dissolving the fort's layout. The psychic waves of Ingrid's thoughts are given permission to transmit. A tumble of whispers. Comets of pure dread. This blank thought canvas fills with Ingrid. Everything within her at this moment is painted upon this canvas in brilliant fluorescence. She is screaming with an intensity the voice cannot contain. The scream extends beyond sound, inventing its own means of conveying the enormity that lives inside. The power weakens Rollo's body as more of his mind is poured into the process of hearing it. His knees meet the ground and his slumped body is close to following suit. Everything in this moment is for Ingrid. She needs help. Something has abandoned her and she is imploding with the pain of that abandonment. Beyond this impossible pain is love. Love denied direction. Denied a home. Rollo wants to build this home and invite Ingrid's love inside. Nurturing it. Allowing expression in order that it may grow.

...

Rollo avoids the Frontal Chamber. He always has. Something unremembered dissuades his entry. Only the rusted habit remains. The habit is controlled by an assumption the Frontal

Chamber is lost to negative energy that will envelop Rollo should he linger within its walls. Ingrid planted a seed that bloomed into this habit, but now it is Ingrid leading him away from that habit and into the Frontal Chamber's walls. Her screams paint arrows that end there. In this moment the habit preventing his entry crumbles and blows away into nothing. The habit means nothing. A habit is tapestry of illusion only afforded importance by our adherence to upholding it.

He runs toward the chamber, toward Ingrid's screaming and tears the entryway apart, throwing the blankets aside where they float down the Medulla Shaft. Rollo stands in the chamber's center and spends a moment studying the demon he turned it into. Beyond Ingrid's encircling screams there is no perniciousness. It is a chamber like the others. Existent, in part, via his hand. It lacks signs of Rollo's day-to-day existence, but feels completely unexceptional. Any reason for Ingrid keeping him out of this space is lost on Rollo. Unless this was a space Ingrid wanted to keep for herself… but why? More importantly, why does it matter? Rollo longs to stop asking questions. He has never asked a question that met the answer it was looking for. Questions will be asked when they are given a path leading to truth. Until then, questions are meaningless.

There is undulation in the walls, like an overweight breeze. It comes and goes, but Rollo sees it. He approaches the movement and places his hand where it occurs. Something solid that does not make a habit of being there. Ingrid's psychic screams have stopped. Even within the machinery's song, all sounds quiet. Ingrid is here. Behind the walls. Trying to get out. Seeking Rollo as he seeks her. He pulls at the blankets, committed to releasing her. To releasing himself. The blankets are not as important as what they hide.

Baby Elephants

A seed planted in the elephant house is given space to become all it wants to be. The elephant house gathers fertility, which it ploughs into the soil, in preparation for the seed's inauguration. The seed is granted passage into this soil where it will remain for up to 700 days. Gestating in the nutrient-rich world prepared for it. A world concerned only with the seed and its needs.

The elephant house permits its seed the time to develop before it feels capable of participating in a world removed from its safety. A gumbo of life allows the seed to understand what it means to think before it is forced to think.

There are five guards who collectively answer to the name Corpus Luteum who devote themselves to the well-being of the seed while it gestates in the elephant house. These Corpus guards take turns. One grows weary and flirts with death before another takes over, destined for the same lifespan. Every action in honor of the blossoming seed. The seed is unaware of the effort given to its protection.

The elephant house will dismantle itself when the seed has become what it needs to be. The resultant growth will eventually help build a new elephant house in honor of the home it once knew. The home that once cared for it so deeply. The house ensures its legacy by caring for those it holds. Being cared for teaches what it means to care. Any seed blossoming from the elephant house is a seed destined to continue a legacy stretching back further than it comprehends.

16.

At first Rollo sees nothing beyond shifting darkness. His eyes strain to adjust, desperate for more visual data. An orb of black glass communicates with outside light, churning it in circles. It glints like a flare fired by someone lost and desperate. Rollo tries to understand how this orb can be Ingrid, determined to make it so.

"Ingrid," he whispers. "I am here."

His words evaporate. The darkness shifts toward solid form Rollo reaches out to touch. Skin touches something that might be skin. Tougher than skin as he understands it, but in possession of qualities married to nothing else. Rollo's fingers explore the tactile phenomena before something nudges them away. He withdraws his hand as though bitten and winces at the emergence of a strange sound, akin to a damaged brass instrument played without skill. The volume is minimal compared to the machinery, but it is new. Whatever this is, it is not Ingrid. A trunk emerges from the darkness, sniffing the air, deciphering the space around it. Rollo is not afraid, and reaches out his hand once more to meet the emergent trunk, which bends toward his palm, covering it in cold wet life.

"I am Rollo," he says.

The trunk tightens around Rollo's hand and tugs, moving his body aside. A baby African elephant shuffles past and stops in the chamber's center. Its ears flap, whisking breeze toward Rollo, cooling the sweat on his brow. The two stare at one another, working to understand this strange moment, remaining locked in this consideration for some time. The elephant's marble eye, enclosed in desert floor cracks of skin, holds answers within. Rollo searches for the questions capable of unlocking these answers. He finds nothing.

The baby elephant's height is smaller than Rollo's, but its overall bulk more imposing. Loose folds of grey skin shift and change with each slight movement, never truly settling into one resting position. Rollo feels compelled to reach his hand toward the elephant once more, but is incapable of doing so. The physicality of the animal deters movement. Instead he remains still, giving the elephant permission to dictate whatever might unfold.

Time passes beyond determination. Rollo believes he can see the elephant growing. Its skin tightening. Trunk lengthening. He assumes illusion, maintaining his role in whatever dynamic is unfolding. Finally. Movement. The elephant lifts its trunk. Reaching it toward the ceiling and stretching it out. Rollo's eyes follow the elevation, training his sight on the trunk's tip, watching it breathe. Growing and shrinking. Preparing to become the point of exit for whatever swells inside.

A burst of water erupts from the trunk, dousing the ceiling above and raining down in thick droplets, bathing Rollo and the chamber. The water intensifies in pressure, forcing the elephant's eyes shut.

Rollo remains still. Arms at his side. Allowing his body to experience the water's enormity. It pools below, filling up the chamber faster than the chamber can cast it out. Lapping at Rollo's ankles. Then shins. Then knees. Creeping up his thighs and toward his waist. When the water level meets the droop of Rollo's breasts the pressure begins to ease. The water eases to a pulse that leaks down the trunk's length. The elephant's eyes reopen and the level begins a slow recession. It thrashes its head from side to side, stands still, and then wades through its eruption. It stops to explore the ground, as if seeking something out. Rollo follows the elephant's path with slow, curious eyes, unaware each time it submerges itself beneath the water, he is holding his breath in sympathy.

The elephant finds an area of floor that owns its focus. It circles this area, making several attempts to forage out whatever interests it so. It tugs and burrows, uprooting blankets, flicking them aside with trunk strokes. In a sudden rush of activity, the sucking sound of a draining sinkhole summons a cincture of water toward the uncovered space. The level lowers. From waist. To thighs. To shins. To ankles. The elephant shakes itself dry and walks toward a corner of the chamber then slumps to its side. Its eyes shut, inviting immediate sleep.

Rollo casts his direction from the sleeping elephant to the newly uncovered area. There is a cavity below floor level he was unaware of. He moves toward it, feeling nervous without understanding why. The cavity is covered in sheets of sodden paper. Each sheet wears handwriting.

The Philosophy of Confession

Confession reconciles self with self. In the absence of God, to whom can one confess if not the self? Who among us does not desire penance when crushed by the weight of our deficiency? It is in deficiency we reside. It is deficiency in command of every breath. Guiding the passage of every thought. We are who we are, in all our individual beauty, because of deficiencies weakening us. Confession reconciles us with, rather than removing us from, our deficiencies.

When dialogue is trapped between self and self, where does our penitent exist but within the self? To avoid destroying this self of ours, in possession of such loathsome deficiency, how do we move forward? Self-expression leads to the garden of reconciliation. Words exist within us ready to find conveyance. Words prepared to hold our deficiencies close. Express everything you hate and feel the power of that hate diminish. Confess everything via the love of words.

Words are divorced from judgment. Offering a discourse with moments of contemplation, almost bewitching the writer into confessions of the deeper self. In the environment of words there is existent the promise of freedom. A place where permission is granted to move away from our everyday entrapment. To embrace deficiency as something integral to the beauty of whom we are. Although born of thought, once written, that which we use words to express enjoys a life separate from the mind. Liberation. Words are often thoughts we lack the courage to convey. Those who keep a diary keep an exploration of something approaching their own truth.

17.

Rollo retrieves a sheet of dampened paper. He studies what is written, understanding the symbols are words. Words are something Rollo has lost connection with, and what he sees resembles abstract shapes. He knows these shapes reach toward a meaning at one point he could understand, and if he could understand them again, answers would be discovered within. He studies the sheet, trying to look into the words rather than through them. Seeking to know what the shapes convey. How each shape forms what he understands to be a letter. How each series of letters combine to become a word. How each word is a package of meaning. How these words, each with their own vast meanings, can be ordered to form strings of new meaning. How these strings of meaning communicate thoughts. Thoughts that can inform existing thoughts. The complexity of the process overwhelms him, threatening to upset any attempt to understand it. After scanning the writing several times, he concludes that two words are familiar. At the top is a word he understands to be his name. It provokes vestiges of unmistakable identity, existing as a package of the self. He allows this word to be recognized. At the bottom of the page is a word he understands to be Ingrid's name. There is a sense he has written this word many times. It is a word he has fought the most to retain and somehow, he has achieved this. Understanding his name appears at the top, and Ingrid's at the bottom, he deduces he is looking at a letter written by Ingrid to him. A letter he does not recall having seen before. It appears this cavity in the chamber floor is a repository for unsent letters. A homage to the continuation of their identities.

At the top-right of each page is something Rollo understands well. A sequence of numbers. In numbers Rollo can comprehend and express the language of the fort, engaging it in dialogue. This sequence of numbers is something he is able to attach meaning to, which may lead to the significance of these letters. Each letter possesses a unique number sequence corresponding to a generic numerical order.

Rollo empties the cavity of each letter until they are strewn about the chamber floor. Once excavated, he begins to sort them based on their simple number sequence. He becomes lost to this task, seeing nothing beyond the numbers until the letters sit in a neat, sodden stack in wait of further exploration.

He stares at the sleeping baby elephant, feeling an inclination to seek its help, but decides against it. Attempting to understand these letters via their words is a process devoid of hope, so he maintains his interest in the numbers and what they suggest. If the numbers are sequential, then they must demarcate the order in which they were written, which means the lower the number, the earlier the letter. By sliding down the number sequence, Rollo may be given an insight to a time he no longer recalls. A record of everything now forgotten exists, and it exists in these impossible words.

He makes his way down the pile of communication, taking in pages of Ingrid's handwriting. Handwriting unique to her, refusing to alter from page-to-page. Neat glyphs that embody Ingrid. She has written volumes. Has conveyed so much thought. All addressed to Rollo, but never intended for him. His journey through her indecipherable thoughts continues, Rollo taking in the patterns and shapes of Ingrid. Appreciating them for what they represent, more than what they are. Then he stops. The significance of what he sees cannot be denied.

18.

About two-thirds into the pile of one-way correspondence, the pattern of Ingrid ceases. He compares the point of caseation with a recent page. The handwriting between the two bears no relationship, as though written by different people. He studies the two words he understands. Rollo at top. Ingrid at bottom. They are still there. A letter addressed to him that could not have been written by Ingrid, but could not have been written by anyone else. His attention shifts back to the number sequence on the top-right. He does not want to admit what seems to grow with increasing clarity inside. He places the letter atop the pile and scrambles toward the cavity. Its base presents several dislodged pencils for Rollo to choose from. He selects one, checking to ensure its tip is sharpened.

Rollo climbs from the cavity. Back toward the letters. Wishing to move beyond them, but understanding he cannot. He feels as though he already knows the answer. Does not want to know the answer. Wishes the answer were something different. He flips a sheet, ignoring the writing on the reverse side, interested only in blank space. The imprint of Ingrid's writing pushes through, insinuating itself. Rollo runs his fingers over the raised reverse like braille before pressing the tip of the pencil against the paper. He examines the number on the top-right of the letter prior to the shift in handwriting and copies it.

17221
17221
17221

17221
17221
17221
17221
17221
17221
17221

Each number repetition possesses the unmistakable idiosyncrasies of Rollo's handwriting. No one else. He compares it with the original. The same unmistakable idiosyncrasies. The handwriting on the page bears similar idiosyncrasies, suggesting the same hand was responsible. His hand. All the letters prior to this one are the same. All were written by Rollo. Letters addressed to himself. Or letters written when he was still himself. When Ingrid was still herself. Letters addressed to whoever Ingrid actually is.

Rollo stands up, leaving the letters behind and moves toward the sleeping baby elephant. He leans against it. The elephant shows no sign of disruption. Rollo feels his body raise and lower in tandem with the elephant's breath. He cups his breasts, studying their reality, massaging them until each nipple releases tiny squirts of colostrum. He feels this fluid drizzle down his body and allows it to soak in.

Rollo understands he is not Rollo. He is in fact Ingrid and Ingrid is Rollo. He is she. She is he. Nothing is as it should be.

...

As teenagers, Rollo and Ingrid met and fell into one another. They each possessed gravity designed for the other's orbit. Gravity no one else could understand. They turned in slow, deliberate circles, giving up everything they were as individuals to become the totality of them. It was not sacrifice. It was evolution. The weaknesses of one empowered by the strengths of the other. A constant process of giving. Sole citizens in their world.

In this dynamic, there was no demarcation between the end of one and the start of the other. They formed a continuous circuit, which cycled the energy responsible for powering their machine. All things must be maintained. Maintenance was redirected toward the fort. The machine responsible for Rollo and Ingrid understood what it meant to suffer, but this suffering went unnoticed. Without intervention, all things move toward their end. The unity of Rollo and Ingrid was no different. Their cracks formed and yawned until these little cracks became an expanse of negative space. This negative space grew hungry. Needed feeding, and was fed, by remnants of their individual pasts. These pasts, until now, had been forgotten to the dynamic of who they were together.

Togetherness slowly pulled away into their pre-together forms. Their identities sought independence once more. Data was sorted and arranged, facilitating Rollo and Ingrid's separation, but this data was incorrect. Rollo's data was attributed to Ingrid's data and vice versa. The extraction of data was so gradual they failed to notice the parts of who they were as individuals being extracted. When the process was over, only the other remained.

...

Should you seek the surface, understand you may never again find the point of submersion.

...

Ingrid holds a scrap of green material against her stomach. A scrap of her baby she wrestled free from the gears. Her passage from the world inside the walls has lacked pace. There is nothing for her to protect anymore. No reason to avoid Rollo. The fort dictated the baby had no place here. Only the fort process to which they have devoted themselves is allowed to matter.

She stares up the Medulla Shaft before traveling further. Before finding Rollo, she craves the Frontal Chamber. A familiar place where she can order her thoughts without engaging anything else. A place she can be in the company of her words. She hopes that Rollo does not see her before she is able to perform this solitary reverie.

The walls of the chamber are soaked with water, but Ingrid pays this little attention. The pools of water acting like a welcome mat at the Frontal Chamber's entry are somewhat difficult to ignore. It is of concern the entrance to her personal space possesses such an alien attribute. Of greater concern is the entryway itself, which has been stripped of its covering. Trepidation requires more energy and acuity than Ingrid can muster, so instead, she steps inside. Her concern is of little concern.

Her letters have been evicted from their home and lay saturated and in waste on the chamber floor. Before this has an opportunity to feed concern, she sees Rollo leaning against a sleeping baby elephant. Rollo is lost in reflection, absent hands caressing his leaking breasts. Ingrid approaches the strange spectacle without fear.

"He is dead," she says.

Rollo breaks away from his private headspace and stares at Ingrid.

"He is dead," she repeats.

"I do not understand."

Ingrid stares at the salvaged scrap of material and passes it to Rollo. He studies it, trying to comprehend its significance. The material has a pattern stitched to its surface. A red circle within a red circle within a red circle.

"That was his name," she says. "Our baby is dead. He fell into the machinery."

The two of them spend some time listening to the clatter around them, still unsure what the machinery is for, but accepting it exists. The sound contains familiarity now, which in itself is comforting.

"I am sorry you did not get to meet him. It is my fault he is dead."

Rollo hands the material scrap back to Ingrid and allows a smile to form.

"You have not done anything," he says. "The baby was never alive."

Ingrid wants to refute this claim. Feels as though she should be insulted, but cannot find it within her. Nothing about the baby was real, and she knows this is so. Any life attributed to the baby was achieved via wishful projection.

"Something happened between us. We have been lost."

Ingrid knows this to be true. It feels right, whatever it is. Something between them has been off-balance. She is incapable of recalling a time when this was not so.

Rollo holds Ingrid's hands in his own, trying to rejoin their broken circuit. Longing to feel the power of what they may have been coursing through them as one. Ingrid pulls the contortion of hands toward her chest, feeding them with the thump of her heart.

"Hi," says Rollo. "I would like to introduce myself. My name is Ingrid."

Ingrid's mouth opens slightly. She stares into Rollo's eyes, longing to understand what they convey. In possession of feeling beyond words. Feeling that can only be understood via feeling. The elephant shows no sign of waking. Rollo's hands grip with greater strength.

"Hi, Ingrid," says Ingrid. "My name is Rollo. It is nice to meet you."

Acknowledgments

To Vanessa.

With thanks to Aditi, Cameron, Ian, Robert, and wool.

About the Author

Matthew Revert is the author of *Basal Ganglia* (Lazy Fascist Press), *How to Avoid Sex* (Copeland Valley/Dark Coast Press), *The Tumours Made Me Interesting* (LegumeMan Books) and *A Million Versions of Right* (LegumeMan Books). Revert has had work published in *Le Zaporogue, The Best Bizarro Fiction of the Decade, In Heaven, Everything Is Fine: Fiction Inspired by David Lynch, The New Flesh,* and *The Bizarro Starter Kit (Purple)*, among others.

www.matthewrevert.com

CPSIA information can be obtained at www.ICGtesting.com
Printed in the USA
BVOW03s1716280414

351936BV00005B/439/P